# FIELD OF DEATH

## *Josef Slonský Investigations*
## *Book Four*

## Graham Brack

SAPERE
BOOKS

# FIELD OF DEATH

Published by Sapere Books.

11 Bank Chambers, Hornsey, London, N8 7NN,
United Kingdom

saperebooks.com

ISBN: 978-1-913028-21-3

# Chapter 1

Josef Slonský sat on the edge of his bed and had a well-deserved scratch to greet the day. He could hear distant church bells greeting Liberation Day on which much of the population would enjoy a day off. For the police, there was no such luxury, because the massed crowds in the centre of Prague meant that a lot of purses and wallets would be liberated too.

8th May, and what a year it had been so far. He could not remember such a concatenation of misery. It started just before Christmas, when Captain Lukas returned from his sick leave minus his misbehaving gall bladder and looking as if he had been given his big brother's uniform.

'You've lost weight, sir,' Slonský had remarked, keen to prove that his observational powers were undiminished.

'Thank you for noticing. About ten kilos, I believe. But since I'm retiring in six months it's hardly worth getting a new uniform.'

'At least buy a new belt, sir, or I'll be having to arrest you for indecent exposure.'

'Yes, they are a bit slack, aren't they? Perhaps a new uniform would be best. I must say, I feel better for losing the weight. I hadn't realised what a difference ten kilos could make. It wouldn't do you any harm to lose a few kilos, Slonský.'

By New Year, Slonský was suspecting a conspiracy. His ex-wife Věra had come round with a book on exercise for the older man. It had some ludicrous title like *Stop Your Belly Sagging* which provoked him to check a few bookshops for retaliatory offerings like *Get Rid Of Droopy Breasts* but there was nothing suitable. She had also given him a pullover for Christmas, which she had noted was 'a bit snug' when he tried it on.

'You must have put some weight on,' she had said. 'I'm sure you were a 102 chest when we were together.'

'That was thirty-seven years ago, woman,' Slonský had growled, but felt obliged to soften his tone when he realised that he had not bought her a present in return. The following day he showed up at her flat with a bunch of flowers, having belatedly screwed up the little "In Loving Memory" card that he had not noticed in the store.

Then February brought one of those moments he thought he would never see. Arriving in a bar to see his old friend Valentin he found the journalist sitting with a glass of clear liquid topped with a slice of lemon.

'What's that?' Slonský asked. 'Vodka?'

'Water.'

'Water? Hadn't they finished washing the glass out when you ordered?'

'No, I ordered a water. Sparkling, of course. I don't want to look like a wimp.'

'Water? You're drinking water? Don't you realise fish pee in that?'

'I'm detoxing.'

Slonský goggled. 'Detoxing? Is there any point at your age?'

'I've been having a bit of liver trouble and the doctor told me to detox. So I have five days of drinking as usual and two with no alcohol at all. Or maybe it's supposed to be the other way round. Anyway, this is one of my two days. And I don't eat any meat on those days either. He told me I need five portions of vegetables a day too.'

Slonský felt that everything he believed in had been overturned. This was simply inconceivable. He and Valentin had been drinking together since they were eleven.

'Hops are a vegetable. So is barley, so that's two. And if you have a litre of beer, that's two portions of each. Get yourself a baked potato and the job's done.'

'They mean green stuff. You know, spinach, broccoli, cabbage.'

It had barely crossed Slonský's mind that you might eat cabbage without pickling it first. Of course, he had heard of vegetarians, but he had never actually met one before. It seemed unpatriotic to him.

Slonský was so nonplussed he missed his mouth with his first slurp and tipped his beer down his tie.

The final insult came from Captain Lukas. There they were, chewing the fat like old colleagues do, when suddenly he came out with it.

'Why don't you come to the gym with me?'

'The gym? Why?'

'To get fit. To tell the truth, I have trouble keeping my weight down. An hour on the machines there helps. Do you know, I haven't felt so good in years! I don't know why I didn't do it before.'

Slonský had half a mind to walk out and send for a psychiatric report on Lukas. You heard about this sort of thing when men got older. They lost their grip.

'You know, Slonský, you could do with getting fitter. I've watched you climbing those stairs. I don't want to hand over to you and find you've had a coronary with the added stress of running the department.'

Slonský's original plan on succeeding Lukas, if it happened, which was by no means certain, had been to give the work to Kristýna Peiperová, but now that the Director of Criminal Police had asked for her to be seconded to him as his new Personal Assistant for a year from 1st June, exactly one month before Lukas left, that was no longer going to be possible.

As part of the application process for Lukas' job Slonský had to submit to a medical, so on 7th May he found himself standing in the doctor's office without a shirt on as the doctor clapped the cold end of his stethoscope to assorted parts of his back and instructed him to breathe deeply.

'According to your weight, Slonský, you should be thirty-eight centimetres taller.'

'Not much I can do about that, doctor.'

'No, so you'd better lose the weight. Around twenty kilos should do it.'

'Twenty? Captain Lukas thought ten.'

'Is he medically qualified? I thought not. No, ten kilos would barely scratch the surface. I doubt people would even notice.'

This came as a shock to Slonský, who thought that losing ten kilos would reduce him to such a skeletal state that passers-by in the street would offer him charity so he could get a decent meal.

'Right, on the treadmill. The target is a kilometre in under nine minutes.'

Slonský took his mobile phone out.

'What are you doing, Slonský?'

'If I have to run a kilometre, I ring for a taxi,' came the reply.

'I'll start it on a slow setting, then speed it up as you get your rhythm.'

Slonský began at a fast walk, but was soon beginning to tire.

'Halfway?' he asked hopefully.

'Three hundred and ten metres. I'll tell you when you're halfway, but you're going to have to speed up a bit, or you won't pass the test.'

'And then?' gasped Slonský.

'If you don't pass, you're not fit for service. You'd get a second test and then retirement on medical grounds.'

Slonský was so astonished that he stopped walking. Sadly the treadmill did not stop, so his feet were carried to the end of the rollers and he was catapulted backwards onto the floor. By great good fortune he banged his head.

'It's best if we scrub this test for today,' said the doctor. 'Come back on the day after the holiday and we'll do it again.'

'Peiperová, I can always rely on you to tell me what you think, can't I?'

'I hope so, sir.'

'Good. Do you think I'm overweight?'

'Do you want a truthful answer or a polite one, sir?'

'Not you too. You Jezebel. Or do I mean Delilah?'

'You could be slimmer, sir. It would do you some good. We'd all like you to be around for a long time to come, so it's good that you even asked the question.'

'It is?'

'It shows you're mentally prepared to contemplate change, sir. It's the first step towards self-improvement.'

Slonský wondered where she had heard this guff. Unfortunately Peiperová interpreted the silent movings of his mouth as evidence of strong emotion, which was right in a way, but the emotion was anger. Feeling that he needed some reinforcement as validation of the change he was contemplating, she knew what was expected of her. She grabbed both his hands, made strong eye contact, and maintained a confident tone of voice.

'You can do it, sir. I have faith in you.'

So after that, he had no choice. Peiperová expected it of him.

Later that day, as Slonský approached the canteen counter, Dumpy Anna lifted the cover off the pastries.

'I can't,' Slonský said miserably. 'I have to lose weight. How am I going to do that?'

Anna indicated her own ample physique. 'Do I look like the sort of person who gives dietary advice?' she said. 'But I'll tell you this. You don't have to give up sausage.'

Slonský's mood lightened at once. 'I don't?'

'No,' she said. 'In moderation, of course.'

'Of course,' agreed Slonský, who thought that five sausages was a moderate portion.

'The thing is,' she continued, 'it's all in the cooking. Meat doesn't have many calories compared with sticky things. It's fat that does it. But if you have your sausage grilled, all the fat runs out, doesn't it? So what's left is basically fat-free.'

'Fat-free sausages? Who'd have thought it?'

Slonský had the sort of smile he had not exhibited since he first discovered that a nice old man brought presents around Christmas.

'Just cut down on bread and pastries. And every time you have a beer, have a glass of water. You'll be skipping around like a mountain goat in no time.'

Thus it was that Slonský woke on Liberation Day or, as he chose to think of it, the first day of the rest of his life. This was not an enticing prospect, and he had stupidly agreed to go to the gym with Captain Lukas. There was not even time to have breakfast, so he threw some old sports clothes in a carrier bag and headed for the police gymnasium.

The first surprise was that Lukas was sitting down. Nobody had mentioned that you could get fit sitting down, but Lukas had one leg on either side of a narrow bench and he was yanking on a couple of handles by his shoulders, swinging them in front of him then letting them recoil. *I could do that*, thought Slonský, but none of those machines was free. There was a rowing machine and, having once rowed as a teenager, he thought he would give that a go. As he recalled, it was the drag of the water on the blade of the oar that made it difficult, but there was no water in the gym so it should be very straightforward.

Slonský perched himself on the seat, bent his knees, and pulled. The resistance of the bar was a surprise to him, and he banged his thigh against the steel strut, which was rather painful. Refusing to give in to a machine, he tried a few more times, and finally managed to put some strokes together. By then Lukas had joined him.

'Good work, Slonský. Believe me, you'll feel the benefit. I'm just going to have a steam bath, but you carry on. Ten minutes of this will be an excellent start.'

As Lukas padded off, Slonský reflected that ten minutes more of this would be a damn miracle. He gritted his teeth and tried to get into some sort of rhythm, because he thought he vaguely remembered once hearing that a steady rhythm made exercise easier.

His attention was caught by a young policewoman who was swinging back and forth on the asymmetric bars. She bounced back off the lower bar, elevated herself to an inverted vertical position, pivoted through a hundred and eighty degrees along the upper bar and dropped back to the lower bar which smacked into her hips, though she showed no sign of wincing, so Slonský did it for her.

'Nice, eh?'

The owner of the voice was standing behind Slonský. The uniform tracksuit betrayed him as a member of the gym staff, though actually the way his singlet clung to his abdominal muscles would have been a giveaway.

'I don't think I've seen you here before,' he said. 'Čada, Ladislav.'

'Slonský, Josef. No, I'm a newbie. My first visit, and possibly my last.'

'Have you been sent?'

'No, but I've got my medical tomorrow and apparently I'm overweight and undertall. Plus I can't run a kilometre in nine minutes, though I reckon that test can't be applied uniformly because there are plenty of people in this building who couldn't do that.'

Čada laughed. 'It's a weed-out test. They use it as a reason to get rid of people. It's only a recommendation anyway. Your line manager can ignore it if you're not one of the Special Operations team. And I don't think you are, somehow.'

'No, nor am I contemplating a career change. Well, you've cheered me up a bit.'

'That's not a reason for not exercising. Hang on, you haven't got that set up for someone of your height. Let me just adjust it a bit.'

Čada tweaked a couple of wheels on the side and flicked a little lever. 'There — try that.'

Slonský rowed again, and found it much easier. 'Thanks, that's a lot better,' he said.

Čada looked around. The little policewoman had finished her routine and headed for the changing rooms. He dropped his voice conspiratorially. 'We can do something about the weight too.'

He fished in the first aid pouch clipped to his waistband and produced a strip of tablets. 'It's an old weightlifter's trick. You take one of these a couple of hours before you weigh in, pee like a waterfall and suddenly you're two or three kilos lighter. After the weigh-in you top up with a couple of glasses of water and you're back to normal in no time. Strictly temporary, of course, but it does the job.'

Valentin was perusing a newspaper when Slonský found him a few hours later.

'I thought Tuesday was one of your alcohol-free days,' he said.

'It is.'

'But it's Tuesday today and unless I'm very much mistaken that's a glass of beer in front of you.'

'It's Liberation Day, Slonský. It would be unpatriotic not to have a drink today.'

'A point well made. I'll join you, just to show Czech solidarity.'

'A word to the wise. They've got a promotion on for one of those beers with juice mixed in. Not a good idea.'

'Do I look like the sort of person who drinks cocktails?'

'No, but they might take advantage of your good nature.'

'Just as well I don't have one, then.'

The waiter brought a couple of beers, since Valentin thought it would be unfriendly not to accept a drink from an old mate, especially on Liberation Day.

'You look like you're enjoying that,' the reporter remarked.

'Last one for a while. I've got to get myself in trim or I risk losing my job.'

'How's that then?' asked Valentin, and Slonský was pleased to note a hint of genuine concern in his voice.

'I've got to have a medical before I get promoted and if I don't pass it, they send a recommendation to my boss to give me the heave on medical grounds.'

Valentin took a long pull from his glass and swilled it around his mouth in thought.

'No problem,' he announced. 'By the time the report gets to Lukas' desk he'll have retired and you'll be in charge. You'll be your own manager, and you can tell them to shove their report where the sun won't fade the ink.'

Slonský managed a weak smile. 'Good try, old friend, but I think in those circumstances they'd send it to the Director. And while I'm reasonably confident that he wants to keep me, and I wouldn't want to upset him, there's a much more serious problem.'

'Oh, and that is?'

'Peiperová says she knows I'll lose the weight. She has faith in me, she says. I can't let her down, Valentin. She looks up to me.'

'Of course she does. You're taller than she is.'

'I meant figuratively looking up to me. And she leaves at the end of the month, so I've got to do some crash dieting.'

'How much have you got to lose?'

'The doctor says twenty kilos.'

'Twenty kilos? Dear God, man, you'll be pure skin and bone. You'll have to wear lead pants or the wind will blow you over.'

'Nevertheless…'

'When were you last twenty kilos lighter?'

Slonský thought for a while. 'I think I was about thirteen. I've always been inclined to the fuller figure, you see.'

'I know. I was around, remember?'

'Well, I'll just have to do the best I can. But a kilo a day will be a tall order.'

Slonský fingered the little strip of tablets in his pocket. They had better be as good as Čada claimed.

# Chapter 2

The morning of day two of the rest of Slonský's life dawned, and his stomach was rumbling from the moment he opened his eyes. His old friend Sergeant Pavel Mucha had told him that a hot drink would fill his innards, so he gulped down two mugs of coffee and then took out the tablets. Reasoning that if the standard dose was one, he probably needed two, he swallowed them with the last of his drink and headed off to the doctor's office for his assessment.

He had not long been in the waiting room when he felt an urgent need to rid himself of the coffee, and was pleasantly surprised to see the volume that he produced. It seemed that, if anything, Čada had understated the effectiveness of these little white tablets. Assuming that they would probably wear off once they had produced an effect, he decided to take another couple while he waited.

'Just sit quietly for ten minutes then I'll take your blood pressure,' said the doctor.

Suiting action to the word, Slonský attempted to sit quietly, but he was acutely aware of accumulating pressure in his bladder and decided he had better pay another visit. Pausing to explain his need to the doctor's receptionist, he found he had to hurry the last few metres and just made it before unleashing his own personal Vltava. When he was quite convinced that the flow had ceased, he gingerly made his way back, though not without careful reconsideration en route, just in case everything was going to erupt again.

The receptionist smiled sweetly at him as he took his seat, then busied herself with renewing the water in the vase of flowers on the windowsill. The steady trickle of fluid from her jug discomfited the old detective, who abruptly left the room once more.

By the time he was invited to enter the consulting room, he was beginning to wonder whether the nine minute test was going to be possible, at least without a comfort break in the middle.

Obediently he stepped onto the scales.

'Excellent,' declared the doctor. 'You've lost four kilos already.'

'Sweat, probably,' said Slonský.

'You've been exercising?'

Slonský was slightly aggrieved at the incredulous tone he thought he detected in the question. 'In the gym yesterday.'

'On Liberation Day? Very conscientious. I'm glad you're taking this so seriously. To be frank, I wasn't sure you were going to engage with us.'

The good humour evidenced suggested to Slonský that merely making the effort counted for something.

'Right, time for the jogging test. Can you manage the kilometre in nine minutes, do you think?'

'I'll do my best,' Slonský replied.

'Good. I'll set it running at a quick walking speed, and when you're ready to step it up just tell me.'

Slonský mounted the treadmill and the belt began to run. He took as much of his weight as possible on the handrests and started to walk as fast as he could. Noting this new-found determination the doctor took it as a hint that the pace was comfortable and therefore increased it a notch. Slonský responded by lengthening his stride and before long was breaking into a jog.

'That's a quarter of the distance and you're just off the pace,' announced the doctor. 'Let's step it up a bit.'

Before Slonský could object he found himself fully occupied in keeping up with the belt and unable to protest because he needed all his puff to keep going. It was at this point that the effect of the unwonted exercise began to stimulate his bladder once again. Realising that the quickest way to get off the treadmill was to speed up and get the wretched kilometre covered, he put on a burst of speed, which provoked the doctor into increasing the velocity of the treadmill. By the time he had covered 750 metres the bladder sensation was very uncomfortable indeed, and Slonský was beginning to worry that he might disgrace himself. *Just let me hang on for a couple of minutes*, he thought. *Try not to think about it*, he told himself, though that was increasingly difficult to do. Suddenly the doctor began counting down.

'Five, four, three, two, one and … stop! Well done, Slonský. Comfortably inside the time.'

'Is the test over?'

'Yes, that's a kilometre.'

'Excuse me.'

Slonský bolted for the door and took off along the corridor.

'If he'd run as fast as that he'd have done it in half the time,' the doctor mused.

As part of a pact of support Officers Jan Navrátil and Kristýna Peiperová had undertaken to try to avoid eating in front of their boss, and were therefore already in the canteen when he returned, polishing off their lunches. Slonský ostentatiously helped himself to a bowl of soup and a roll, and came to sit beside them.

Peiperová felt the need to demonstrate her role as chief cheerleader.

'You're doing very well, sir,' she said.

'Aren't I?' agreed Slonský. 'I've just passed my medical with flying colours, including completing a kilometre in seven minutes, fifty-three seconds.'

Navrátil was impressed and said so.

'I've also lost four kilos. At this rate I shall soon be transparent, though not as transparent as the look of incredulity on your face, lad.'

'Sorry, sir. I'm not disbelieving, just pleasantly surprised. I must admit I thought you'd find it more difficult than this.'

'Iron willpower, Navrátil. That's what you're seeing in action.' Slonský indicated the folded newspaper at Navrátil's right hand. 'Anything happened in the world today?'

'Unrest in a country I've never heard of somewhere near the Black Sea. There's a bit about that explosion yesterday.'

'What explosion?'

'Didn't you see it on the news? Some of those people who go out with metal detectors found a World War II bomb. Unfortunately it exploded and killed them.'

'Where was this?'

'Somewhere near Holice, on the main road to Pardubice.'

'Poor devils. It's an odd place to find stuff from the war.'

'Why, sir? The Germans went past, the Germans came back, the Russians came through. Any of them could have left unexploded bombs behind.'

'True. But it's not an unpopulated area. It's just surprising that nobody found it before. And when they say it was a bomb, are they being literal, or could it have been a shell?'

Navrátil unfolded the paper and scanned the article. 'It doesn't say.'

'No, but it matters. You see, loose language is the enemy of detection. Now, what are you two doing today?'

Peiperová spoke first. 'I'm dealing with that domestic violence case, sir. The wife still won't implicate either her husband or her son.'

'We need to sort that out, lass. Even if nobody else knows who did it, the three of them do, and whichever male didn't do it will have the other one if we're not careful. It's only the fact that one or other has been here that has prevented that.'

'The son went home this morning.'

Slonský paused with his spoon hovering in mid-air. 'Shame. We should have gone with him to hear what was said when he got there. Perhaps you can engineer a pretext to go out and check a bit of a statement, just to see how things are lying.'

Peiperová nodded

'Now would be good,' Slonský added.

Peiperová nodded again.

'And you?'

'Burglary at Karlín, sir.'

'Excellent. Well, since the chances that the burglars will hide their stash here are pretty low, perhaps you'd better go somewhere else to look for them, don't you think?'

Navrátil reluctantly agreed, while wondering whether Slonský's snappishness was a consequence of his dieting. Slonský was thinking the same thing himself, but since regret was not a feeling that occupied him very often or for very long, he soon put it to one side and got on with reading the little handbook that was essential reading for all officers of the rank of captain and above, if Human Resources were to be believed.

He was absorbed in "How to Lead a Successful Team" when he realised that he was no longer alone. Glancing up from the book he found himself gazing into the bloodhound eyes of Sergeant Mucha.

'Didn't see you arrive,' he explained.

'Obviously. Are you all right?'

'All right? Yes. Why shouldn't I be all right?'

'I have been deputed, as your oldest and closest friend in this building, to find out why you're behaving like a bear with piles.'

'I'm not.'

'You're outvoted about fifty to one on that one.'

'I'm my normal self.'

'Exactly — a bear with piles. But more so than usual. If this is what becoming a captain does to you, let it go. We'd rather have the crusty old curmudgeon we know and love, without having you biting everyone's head off as an optional extra.'

Slonský considered this a moment. 'This isn't a wind-up?'

'No.'

'You really feel I'm being hard on people?'

'Yes.'

'You personally — my oldest and, up to now, closest friend here?'

'Yes.'

Slonský refolded Navrátil's newspaper slowly and rose from his seat. 'Tough,' he said.


Slonský was back in his office when the telephone rang. It turned out to be Dr Novák, the pathologist, for whom Slonský had a lot of respect though, of course, it would not do to let him know that.

'That explosion at Holice,' Novák began. 'Did you see it in the papers?'

'No, I didn't. Nor on the television, nor on the radio, nor tattooed on my backside while I was asleep. Why?'

'There's something odd about it. I've been at the site all morning and I think you should take a look at this.'

'It's not my case.'

'Well, whose case is it?'

'It isn't anyone's case. It's not a crime.'

'I think it might be,' said Novák, 'but I need an experienced policeman to tell me so.'

Reluctantly Slonský agreed to drive over to Holice, and since he disliked driving, this meant selecting one of his team to act as chauffeur. The short straw was selected for Peiperová, who drove back to collect Slonský and take him along the road.

'No point disturbing Navrátil when he's only just started work on the Karlín thing,' Slonský explained.

Peiperová opened her mouth to protest but decided not to do so. Slonský occasionally needled one of them to see whether their romantic relationship was affecting their objectivity. In fact, they were being highly professional about it all, and kept it strictly out of the office.

They pulled in opposite the entrance to a field and strode through the open gate. Peiperová had boots in the back of the car, whereas Slonský had to make do with some disposable overshoes.

Novák was standing to the left of the field which was basically rectangular. To the right of the gate were some thick bushes, or possibly sawn-off trees that screened much of the field from view. There was a crater about twenty metres into the field around which four bodies lay under sheets of blue plastic.

'They're still here?' asked Slonský.

'Yes, because I wanted you and Professor Brandl to see them in situ, so we erected a tent over them last night.'

Novák introduced a slight, dapper man who could well have walked out of the nineteenth century. Brandl wore a three-piece suit with a large gold chain looping across the front, and had a neat silver beard. Since much of his moustache was still black this gave him a slightly strange appearance.

'Professor Brandl is a renowned international authority on blast injuries,' Novák explained.

*If he is so renowned how come I've never heard of him*, thought Slonský, but said nothing.

'I invited him to have a look at the site and he concurs with my opinion, but I'll let him explain,' Novák continued. 'Professor?'

Brandl squatted and pulled back the ends of the blue sheets nearest the crater. It was not a pretty sight.

'As you can see, all the men suffered serious leg injuries.'

'Well, if they were standing by a shell when it went off, they would,' Slonský replied in his most reasonable tones.

'Ah, just so; but there are two cogent reasons for doubting that explanation,' the professor continued. 'First, the seats of their trousers were muddy. They had been sitting in the mud. Why would they do that when there are two large logs just a few paces away?'

'That's a fair question,' Slonský conceded.

'And the second reason,' Brandl continued, 'is that they somehow contrived to explode a shell when their hands were tied together.'

'What?'

'You'll see here — this is the best example, but they all have it to some degree — that the skin around the wrists has been cut into by something quite narrow. And Dr Novák here will show you why.'

*Quite the little double act*, thought Slonský.

Novák produced a clutch of transparent evidence bags, in each of which was something that looked like two or three centimetres of black worm.

'Cable ties, plastic. What would they be doing in a field, I wonder? My suspicion is that the men were killed, then someone came back to remove the ties, but he didn't find all the pieces in the mud.'

'Were they dead before the explosion?' asked Slonský.

'We doubt it,' Novák answered. 'We both think they were alive when the bang went off. There was substantial arterial blood spray indicative of beating hearts. One or two might have been killed by the explosion, but a couple of them bled to death from their wounds.'

Slonský circled the grisly scene.

'Paint a picture for me, Novák. What am I looking at here?'

'My best guess — and it is just a guess — is that the men were tied up and made to sit on the ground. Perhaps their ankles were also tied and those are among the pieces of cable tie we found. They were positioned in a cross with their feet meeting at the centre. Then someone lobbed a grenade into the middle.'

'Jesus Maria!' exclaimed Slonský quietly.

Peiperová, who was possessed of an abnormally strong stomach, peeled back the cover from one of the victim's faces. It was blackened on one side and there were slashes in the skin where small metal fragments had sliced into it.

'Do we know who they are, sir?'

'Yes,' answered Novák, 'the local police know them all. One of them is a policeman himself, the local lieutenant in the criminal branch. The uniformed chief has told the families. They probably guessed, of course, when their men didn't come home last night.'

'Time of the explosion?' Slonský snapped.

'It was heard just before six o'clock last evening,' Novák said. 'Getting time of death from these bodies would be pretty tricky.'

Slonský thanked them curtly and was about to move away when Novák stopped him.

'There's something else you may want to see.'

He led them to the lower edge of the field where it butted against the road. There were two parallel gouges in the ground there.

'A lorry?'

'The tracks are too wide, Slonský. And too heavy, I think. But whatever was here wasn't moved that long ago. In fact, you'll see the ground is quite dry in the centre. The rain yesterday morning didn't reach that bit of ground.'

Slonský nibbled his lower lip.

'I ought to have been more suspicious when they said four men with metal detectors had blown themselves up. If anyone ought not to be killed by unexploded shells in the ground it's people who have metal detectors. So, something big was here yesterday, but it's not today. And four men were murdered in the same field.'

He beckoned to Peiperová to follow him as he walked out of the field towards the road.

'There are tracks through the gate, sir.'

'Yes, but not as deep because it was moving quite quickly and didn't sink in as much as when it was stationary. But that's not what I want to know. You go that way and I'll go this. I want to know in which direction it went.'

Peiperová began to walk towards the village while Slonský ambled back towards the road from which they had turned off. He had almost reached the road when he found what he was looking for, and whistled to Peiperová to join him.

'Look!' he exclaimed. 'It couldn't quite make the turn so the back wheels ran over the verge.'

'That's not a standard tyre tread,' said Peiperová. 'What is it?'

'I don't know,' said Slonský, 'but we need to find out.'

# Chapter 3

Captain Forman slurped his coffee which was being supported by his ample belly.

'It's awful,' he said, for the umpteenth time.

'Awful,' echoed the mayor.

'That such a thing could happen in our village!' added Veselý, the deputy mayor who, despite his name, was anything but cheerful.

Peiperová sat with her pencil poised, waiting to capture anything helpful that the three local worthies said, except that in the first fifteen minutes of the meeting they had said nothing useful of any kind.

Slonský gave them some encouragement. 'Describe the victims to me so I get as complete a picture as possible of these men.'

Each looked at the others before the mayor decided it was his duty to speak.

'Let's start with Lieutenant Sedlák. He was fifty-eight, I think, a man with an excellent police record — though no doubt you already know that — married, no children that I know of. Jakub Lacko, fifty-three, an engineer, and his son Pavel, who was about twenty-six. And then there was the chairman of the detectors' club, Karel Procházka. He was in his forties and ran a motorbike repair shop in Pardubice.'

Slonský had never heard of Sedlák, but on reflection he realised that he had never heard of any policeman from the Pardubice region. They liked to keep themselves to themselves and rarely asked for help. Nonetheless, as a fellow criminal policeman he thought he ought to know him.

Forman pointed to a picture of a man receiving some sort of certificate from the mayor.

'That's Sedlák.'

Ah, thought Slonský, *that* Sedlák! Mr Anonymous Bore-The-Pants-Off-Everyone-Else Sedlák.

'Good copper,' said the mayor. 'Got the crime rate right down.'

Slonský was about to suggest that this had been achieved by simply not bothering to report any crime when he decided that you can't speak ill of the dead.

'I don't know what we'll do without him,' agreed Forman.

'The field where it happened,' Slonský said. 'Do you know who owns it?'

Forman glanced to the others for support. 'I don't think so.'

'Well, could you find out?' hissed Slonský.

'It might be difficult,' Forman replied. 'Nobody came forward to say it was their field.'

'The gate was recently oiled,' interjected Peiperová, 'so somebody has been going there.'

'I'll ask about,' said Forman.

'Can you think of anyone who might have a grudge against these men?' Slonský enquired.

'No,' said the mayor. 'People around here aren't ones for grudges. Live and let live, that's our motto.'

'Perhaps someone Sedlák put away?'

'I doubt it,' offered Forman. 'I can't remember when Sedlák last arrested anyone.'

'There were those boys who were selling cars that had been written off by the insurers,' suggested Veselý.

'But where would they get a grenade?' asked the mayor.

'Maybe they found it,' Veselý proposed.

'There can barely be a metre of field Procházka and his mates haven't already checked over with their gadgets,' the mayor answered.

'Then why were they out?' Slonský asked. 'If they've already been everywhere, what were they looking for?'

The meeting drew to a close and Slonský stomped out to the car, climbed in and slammed the door behind him. Peiperová found him with his lips pressed hard together as if he were suppressing some great emotion.

'Are you all right, sir?'

'If we could go back through time to the days of the neanderthals, Peiperová, that lot would feel right at home. God, the long winter nights must just fly by there! If I lived in that village I'd run amok. I wouldn't be responsible for my actions.'

'You must try to keep calm, sir. It's not good for your blood pressure.'

'Keep calm? With that bunch? Jesus Christ himself couldn't keep calm with them. If they were his disciples he'd splat them with a bolt of lightning and say "Stuff it, I'll manage with nine." Jesus Maria!'

They drove back towards Prague, Slonský interrupting the silence at intervals to rage at inefficient public officials, and then telling Peiperová to stop at a pub beside the road before they had gone very far.

'I need a drink. Come on, lass, I'll break the habit of a lifetime and buy you one.'

'I'm in uniform, sir.'

'Well, take it off. Not all of it, obviously,' he added hurriedly, 'but your jacket.'

'The shirt is police issue too, sir.'

'Peiperová, stop being difficult. You can have a coffee, can't you? Even the police are allowed coffee on duty, thank God. And why are you in uniform anyway?'

'I had to see the Director of Criminal Police this morning, sir. They call it orientation.'

'Upright and facing him is the best bet,' Slonský replied.

It was quiet in the bar as Slonský ordered the drinks and sat on one of the barstools. The barman eyed up Peiperová's uniform.

'You'll be here about the big bang, then.'

'Hear it from here, did you?' asked Slonský.

'Oddly enough, no. You'd have thought we would have done, because it's not that far and it was a still evening.'

Slonský took a pull at his beer. 'That's nice, that is. Got any sausages?'

Peiperová sighed inwardly. Once Slonský had beer and sausage the chances of an early evening return to Prague went out of the window.

'As it happens, we have. Locally made. A couple each?'

'Why not?' beamed Slonský. 'If she doesn't want them I'm sure I'll make room.'

'Remember your diet, sir,' whispered Peiperová.

'Then eat both of yours and save me from myself,' Slonský whispered back.

When they returned, Slonský pushed open the door of police headquarters and was delighted to see that Sergeant Mucha was on shift.

'You're here late,' he said.

'The wife's sister invited herself for a few days.'

'My commiserations.'

'No matter. I have to do a few late shifts sometimes, just to show willing.'

Mucha managed the roster for the front desk and unaccountably seemed always to be on duty when his sister-in-law (also known as The Evil Witch of Kutná Hora) came to stay. He had never admitted to his wife that he devised the off-duty rota, blaming his antisocial hours on Sergeant Varkan, an argument that would have held more weight if Varkan had not died five years earlier.

'Tell me, old friend, how can I find out who owns a piece of land?'

Mucha leant forward and lowered his voice. 'Would this be a piece of land on the edge of Holice where a certain explosion took place yesterday?'

'The very same.'

'Then that's easy,' Mucha replied. 'It's owned by an old woman called Valachová.'

'Are you winding me up or do you actually know?'

'The cheek! Would I impede an investigation with dodgy information?'

'Yes. You've done it before.'

'Well, yes,' admitted Mucha, 'but not one of yours.'

'That's true.'

'It really is a woman called Irina Valachová.'

'How do you know this?'

Mucha leaned forward again. 'It's like this. You remember you drove to Holice today?'

'Yes. I'm not ga-ga.'

'And you remember meeting Novák in the field?'

'Yes. Get on with it.'

'And then you had a coffee somewhere?'

'At the police station. How do you know I had a coffee?'

31

'Because you always do. Well, while you were waffling to our colleagues there, your driver was busy phoning her boyfriend on her mobile to tell him to find out who owned the field. He did, and when he went home he told me.'

'Did he, indeed? I'll have words with him. He was supposed to be sorting out a burglary in Karlín.'

'He did that too, straight after lunch. Cell six, if you want a word with them too.'

There were two serious deficiencies in the Human Resources department of the Czech Police, according to Slonský. First, they were a bunch of clockwatchers who went home as soon as the clock struck whatever hour it was when they were due to go home. Slonský was unsure when exactly that was, but it was before seven, which was the time when he preferred to raise any queries he had about his fellow officers. Second, they were so lacking in basic security awareness that they had completely failed to notice that Slonský had a duplicate key to their document store. Mucha had one too, but his was authorised, because if there were a fire out of hours the desk sergeant had to have a way of getting in to preserve the records. Mucha's key was safely locked in the office safe, but one lunchtime it had been allowed out for a little jaunt in the company of Slonský and had come back with a twin.

This twin was inserted into the lock and deftly turned by a gloved hand. Of course, if there were a legitimate evidentiary need Slonský could have requested Sedlák's file through official channels, but until he had read it he did not know whether he needed to request it, which would involve him in all sorts of tedious paperwork. No, his was much the better way, he decided, as he closed the door and sat on the floor so that he could not be seen through its glazed upper half.

It was dark in the room but he could not switch on a light in case someone passed by, so he produced a small flashlight from his pocket and settled down to read.

Sedlák, it seemed, was an exemplary officer. Even his file was dull. No scandal attached to his name; there were not even any disciplinary hearings listed there, unlike Slonský's own folder which included a lengthy list of misdemeanours — or had done before Slonský got his duplicate key. Slonský had been sensible about it, and had only abstracted one leaf, but that was enough to keep it within reasonable bounds.

He returned the folder to its place, closed the filing cabinet, looked out into the corridor cautiously, then slipped out and locked the door behind him. He smiled at his own cunning, and was just putting the key back in his pocket when he heard a voice behind him.

'What were you doing in there?'

'I wish you wouldn't creep up on people like that,' Slonský grumbled.

'Sorry, sir, but it's just as well it was me and not Lieutenant Doležal,' Navrátil answered.'

'Doležal? Is he in the building?'

'Working late on an attempted blackmail.'

'Who is he attempting to blackmail? And how did you know I was here? Have you tagged my clothing?'

'You left the drawer open. The secret drawer in which you keep your secret key.'

'Not so secret now, evidently. Who else knows?'

'We haven't said anything, sir.'

'We? Don't tell me, Little Blue Riding Hood knows too.'

'Her lips are sealed, sir.'

'For now, Navrátil, for now. But if I know women, one day I'll speak severely to her and she'll squeal.' An awful thought struck him. 'Just a couple of weeks from now she'll be working for the Director of the Criminal Police, lad. I'd best find somewhere else for it. Have you got one of those little ledges inside your desk?'

'I'm not keeping it.'

'Why not? She won't turn you in. You're her boyfriend.'

'It's a dismissable offence, sir.'

'Only if you're caught, Navrátil. And you're a clever lad — you won't get caught.'

'No, sir! I'll keep the secret but I won't keep the key.'

'All right, keep your voice down. Why are you here anyway? Mucha told me you'd left.'

'I was going to call on Kristýna at the barracks, sir, but then I thought you might be here and I could tell you about the burglary in person.'

'Burglary?'

'The one at Karlín, sir. The one you sent me to solve.'

'Ah, that burglary. I hear you did well.'

'They're downstairs in cell six, sir.'

'So I understand. What put you on to them?'

'The fact that when I got there the victims of the crime were busily carrying all the stolen stuff back up the stairs to their flat.'

'That's helpful of them.'

'Yes, sir. They also had some items from another flat including a very distinctive table lamp in the form of a silver lady dancer.'

'Very similar to the table lamp in the form of a silver lady dancer reported stolen from that flat in Josefov?'

'Exactly like it, sir.'

'And do the gentlemen have any explanation for this?'

'No, sir. They're waiting for their lawyer to think of one.'

'That's what we pay lawyers for, Navrátil. Don't let me keep you from your night of passion, lad.'

'We're going to the cinema, sir.'

'Again? Haven't you seen all the films ever made by now? Or don't you look at what's on the screen?'

'Sir! Officer Peiperová and I have never…'

'Joke, Navrátil, joke.'

Slonský skipped down the stairs to his office and had just fixed the key to the inside of Peiperová's desk with sticky tape when there was a knock on the door and Lieutenant Doležal entered without waiting to be invited.

'Slonský, I just — what are you doing?'

'Me? Oh, Peiperová has been complaining that her desk drawer was catching on something.'

'Do you want me to take a look?'

'It's fixed! Look.'

Slonský slid the drawer quickly in and out, demonstrating that it was indeed catching on something, but since Doležal could not see clearly he got away with it.

'Did you want something, Doležal, or did you just come to sneak around my office?'

'Certainly not!'

Doležal appeared outraged. Since he was generally a seriously uptight man, he did outrage particularly well. Slonský attributed this to the fact that Doležal was a notorious teetotaller. It was rumoured that he owned not one, but *two* complete sets of Bruckner symphonies, prompting Slonský to question whether this was a recognised psychiatric condition. His black moustache quivered with indignation until he realised that he could hardly maintain this attitude given the purpose of his visit.

'No, I came in the hope of a quiet, off-the-record chat before you assume your new duties.'

'My duties as captain, you mean?'

Slonský had noticed that Doležal appeared to be incapable of voicing the word "Captain" in association with the name "Slonský". That was probably a recognised psychiatric condition too.

'Yes. Congratulations again, by the way.'

The appointment of Slonský had only been in doubt because Slonský himself did not want the job. He had accepted the promotion only because he could not bear the thought of either of the other lieutenants, Doležal or Dvorník, being placed over him. It might have been a difficult decision for the Director of Police, since Doležal had the advantage in length of service but Dvorník had a personal armoury that would have been the envy of many small police stations.

'Thank you.'

'I just wondered whether you were thinking of appointing a senior lieutenant to replace you.'

Slonský had not considered this possibility, and now that it had been dropped into his lap he foresaw a range of opportunities, all of which would keep Lieutenants Doležal and Dvorník in abject submission so long as he did not actually make a decision.

'It would be premature for me to think about that before I take up the position formally,' Slonský replied. 'But I'm grateful for your interest. Ask me again after 1st July.'

Doležal seemed to consider this as some level of commitment and went away happily, leaving Slonský to ponder who might be appointed as the third lieutenant whom he could reasonably prefer to Doležal and Dvorník.

# Chapter 4

When morning came Slonský could not help noticing that something was missing.

'You gave her the morning off to choose a retirement present for Captain Lukas, sir,' Navrátil reminded him.

Slonský nodded regretfully. Since her arrival a little over a year ago Peiperová had been the self-appointed social secretary of the department, tirelessly trudging from room to room to collect for birthdays, christenings — Dvorník seemed to keep up a never-ending demand for those — or leaving presents. And now she was leaving herself, allegedly just for a year, to go and skivvy for the Director of Criminal Police. This had necessitated some forward planning with Peiperová being deputed to make the arrangements for Lukas' leaving do although she would actually be leaving first.

'She's got plenty to work with,' Navrátil assured him. 'She says people have been very generous.'

'I wonder how much they'll collect for me when I go,' Slonský murmured.

'You'd best hang on till Officer Peiperová comes back, sir. She's very good at getting a few extra crowns here and there.'

'I'm sure she is. She's a very persuasive young woman. How much did she get out of you?'

'It's confidential, sir!'

'I know. I'm just trying to gauge how much I should put in.'

'You haven't given?'

'I can't have been around when she was collecting. So, how much?'

'If you must know, sir, five hundred crowns.'

'Five…! He's got a pension, Navrátil. He doesn't need a lump sum from you.'

'The Captain has been really good to me, sir. And he's a nice man.'

Slonský nodded dumbly. You could not argue with that. He fished in his wallet for a thousand crowns and put it in an envelope on Peiperová's desk. Navrátil left to fetch some coffee and Slonský briefly toyed with the idea of taking five hundred crowns back, but decided that Lukas deserved it. In fact, he deserved more, but there are limits. *I'll miss him*, thought Slonský. *Damn it.*

The day took a sudden turn for the better when Lukas spotted Slonský passing his door and invited him in.

'You'd best close the door behind you,' said Lukas. 'People here are terrible eavesdroppers.'

*They're actually very good at it*, thought Slonský, but said nothing.

'The thing is, Slonský, that one of our men was killed in the explosion at Holice.'

'I know, sir. I'm investigating it.'

'So you are. Well, the local station needs a new lieutenant. I've told them we can't spare anyone. Then it occurred to me that the one person here who isn't doing much is me. I could go there for a few weeks while they recruit someone else.'

'But you're a captain, sir, and they're after a lieutenant.'

'True, but they won't be charged the difference in salary. And it would give you a free hand.'

Slonský was concerned by this development. He had, for once, given a bit of thought to the future and had earmarked a few changes he planned to make, but this threatened to derail his schemes. He had to think quickly.

'You're indispensable, sir,' he announced.

'No, I'm not, and you know it. I'm going in about six weeks anyway, so let's not try to pretend I'm needed.'

'As an example, sir.'

'Well, thank you, but I doubt that too.'

Slonský's brain was firing on all cylinders when an idea came to him. Assuming an expression of the deepest reluctance, he began to stammer the real reason. 'It's Peiperová, sir.'

'Peiperová? How so?'

'She's set her heart on giving you the mother of all send-offs. I shouldn't be saying this, but she's worked tirelessly on the plan for your leaving do.'

Lukas looked abashed. 'I had no idea. Really?'

'You're very well-loved, sir. Do you know, she was telling me that the collection for your gift has been the largest we've ever had in this building?'

'Goodness me! I don't know what to say.'

Lukas pulled out a large, impeccably pressed handkerchief and blew his nose loudly before dabbing at the corner of each eye in turn.

'Of course, we all know that your preference would be just to slip quietly out of the back door with the minimum of fuss, but they would be so disappointed if you weren't here so they can say goodbye properly.'

'I can't deny that I'm not good with ceremony, Slonský, but it would be cruel to spoil Peiperová's efforts by selfishly going away.'

Slonský judged that the moment was right to strike. 'Besides, sir, I have a better idea. When I take over, we'll need a senior lieutenant. I thought perhaps this was a good opportunity to let Doležal spread his wings a bit. He's been here a long time and

I think perhaps he needs somewhere other than Prague to develop his skills fully.'

Slonský resisted the considerable temptation to add "if any" after "skills".

'Do you know, Slonský, I think you've got something there. We'll never find out what Doležal can do so long as he has one of us to shelter behind. I'll go and have a word with him right now.'

'You're in a good mood, sir,' Peiperová exclaimed when she returned to the office.

'And well I might be, lass. Doležal is being posted to Holice as their temporary criminal lieutenant.'

Navrátil immediately spotted a potential flaw in Slonský's plan. 'Won't he expect to take over the explosion case, sir?'

'Eh?'

'As the local ranking criminal policeman, sir, won't he think it's his case?'

'But we've already started it, Navrátil.'

'It's not as if we've made much progress, sir.'

'Well, lad, he doesn't start till Monday, so it's up to us to make lots of progress before then, isn't it?'

Slonský left the office to meet Valentin and found him glugging a mouthful of water.

'Honestly, it's not bad when you get used to it,' he said.

'Like banging your head on a wall is okay when you stop,' said Slonský.

'I can have a drink at the weekend.'

'Roll on the weekend, then.'

'Amen to that, brother.'

'Valentin, do you know anyone who knows about military stuff?'

'Military? Well, we both did national service.'

'Yes, but I was thinking more technical.'

Valentin scratched his chin. 'I might. Our defence correspondent was a bright lad.'

'Was?'

'He left last year to go and work for a think-tank.'

'Is he discreet?'

'Goes with the job. You can't get people to talk to you if you're known to blab.'

'You do.'

'Ah, but only to you. Otherwise I'm the soul of discretion.'

'Can you fix up a meeting?'

'How soon?'

'Soon as you like. I've got a puzzle and I can't make any progress till someone gives me a steer.'

Valentin fished a phone from his pocket and began searching his contacts.

'How long have you had that?' Slonský asked.

'This? A couple of years, I suppose.'

'I've never seen it before.'

'It's a work phone. When I meet you I'm off duty.'

'You've never given me your number,' Slonský complained.

'You've never asked.'

'Well, I wouldn't, would I, if I didn't know you had one. How was I meant to know?'

'You're a detective,' Valentin answered. 'You should have detected it.'

Valentin's man Kohoutek was free, intrigued, and quite close at hand, so within the hour he was sitting opposite them sipping a half-litre of beer. He was in his mid-thirties, possessed of woolly chocolate brown hair that merged into a woolly brown beard, and severe black-rimmed glasses of a type that Slonský thought had gone out of fashion in the sixties.

He lifted the photograph of the vehicle tracks up to the light, used his thumb to measure off some distances and looked remarkably excited for a man who was looking at a picture of a muddy field.

'Holice, did you say?'

'That's right,' agreed Slonský.

'Where the explosion was?'

'I didn't mention any explosion.'

'I know you didn't. But I'm asking.'

'Not far away.'

'Do you know what caused the explosion?'

Slonský hesitated. 'Why do you ask?'

Kohoutek checked the table was dry before putting the photograph down carefully.

'Because people with experience of metal detectors are unlikely to set off anything big enough to kill four of them, so the story in the press is bull.'

'Between us?'

Kohoutek nodded.

'The likely explanation is that the four men were tied up, placed in a circle, and someone exploded a grenade between them.'

'Dear God!' exclaimed Valentin.

Kohoutek simply nodded a few times. 'That figures. Have you got the fragments of grenade?'

'The technicians are looking at them.'

Kohoutek rocked back in his chair, removed his glasses and gave them a slow polish before carefully replacing them on his nose. 'I have a story to tell you but I can't vouch for any of it. I first heard it many years ago but I never believed it until now. Has either of you heard of the Ghost Battery?'

'You mean like white sheets and woo-woo-woo?' asked Slonský.

'That would be the derivation, but they were allegedly very real. In 1968 the rest of the Warsaw Pact invaded our country. The Czechoslovak Army was ordered by Prague not to resist, and to lay down all their weapons. According to the story, the Heavy Artillery Regiment at Pardubice got those orders like everyone else, but the commander decided that if he did that the country would be utterly defenceless. On the other hand if he openly rebelled the immense Warsaw Pact army could soon deal with him. So the colonel — a man called Bosák — detached one self-propelled gun and a team of four men and told them to take it away and hide it somewhere.'

'Hide a gun? I've seen them — they're huge. How could you hide one of those?'

'That's why I didn't believe it. But bear with me a minute till I finish the story. Bosák could do this because a Soviet armoured division had a fixed complement of men and guns, but they knew that their Warsaw Pact allies quite often varied this, so when the Heavy Artillery Regiment was stood down by the Soviets they were not at all suspicious when they counted the materiel and personnel.'

'I can buy that,' agreed Slonský. 'It's such a daft idea I don't think I'd be suspicious either.'

'The four men were told to lose their uniforms and slip back into civilian life, and Bosák removed them from regimental records, at least so far as he could.' Kohoutek took a slurp from his beer and ruffled his hair before continuing. 'I interviewed Bosák just before he died, and he wouldn't confirm or deny the story. There have been hints from one or two of his subordinates, but nothing concrete to follow up. So I worked through the regimental records trying to find out who the four crew men must have been, but I couldn't — they were in too much of a mess. I suppose that was suspicious in itself, because normally army records are near perfect. Anyway, I had no idea whether the story was true or not, or where that missing gun had got to, if indeed it ever existed.' Kohoutek picked up the photograph. 'But now I know, Lieutenant, because I'm looking at a set of self-propelled gun tracks.'

Lukas was concerned to hear the latest turn of events. 'I'm concerned, Slonský,' he said. 'Very concerned. Aren't you concerned?'

'Of course, sir. We don't want ordinary citizens driving around the country with a thumping big piece of artillery, do we?'

'That's exactly why I'm concerned,' Lukas explained.

'But why, sir?'

'Isn't it obvious, man? Think of the damage they could do…'

'Sorry, sir, you misunderstand me. I meant to ask why anyone would keep a forty year old military antique. And if the murders are related to the presence of the hardware, why would they kill to keep it secret?'

'Presumably they have ammunition?'

'According to Dr Kohoutek, there was ammunition stored when the gun was hidden.'

'But won't it have deteriorated?'

'That depends on how it was stored, sir, but we know they won't have left it sitting around in the open, so it may well be in good condition.'

'What about the vehicle itself, Slonský?'

'Kohoutek says it's quite simple mechanically. Someone who had time to familiarize themselves with it could keep it going until they needed spare parts. His guess is that to save wear and tear they probably just turned the engine over now and again and rolled it back and forth to check the brakes haven't seized. If it's in a barn or hangar it may never have needed to go outside.'

'So why was it outside now?'

'I don't know, sir. It's yet another thing I'll have to find out.'


Peiperová had been despatched to track down Mrs Valachová, the owner of the field. She had an address that Navrátil had found from the public records, but Mrs Valachová was out. Enquiry at the small grocery brought forth the suggestion that Irina Valachová was probably either having a chat with her friend who ran the dressmaking business or cleaning the church. Peiperová tried the church first, and found a tiny woman sitting on the steps in front of the altar as she polished the candlesticks.

'Mrs Valachová?'

'Miss.'

'I'm sorry?'

'It's Miss Valachová. I'm not married.'

'Oh, I'm sorry.'

'Don't be. From what my friends tell me I haven't missed much. But then perhaps you're married and know otherwise?'

'No, I'm not. At least not yet. I'm Officer Peiperová from the police in Prague.'

Miss Valachová inspected the proffered identification. 'I've been to Prague,' she announced. 'We went to the ballet. Some of my friends organised it for my sixtieth birthday. It was wonderful.'

'It must have been,' agreed Peiperová.

'4th October, 1975,' added the old lady.

'You're ninety-one?'

'Don't tell everyone! I like to keep a bit of mystery about myself. Is this about the explosion?'

'I'm afraid so.'

'Well, don't just stand there, girl. Sit beside me and grab a cloth. There's a lot of brass to polish.'

Peiperová rolled back her sleeves and did as she was told.

'Not too much polish, mind. You only have to rub it off again when it's done its work.'

'Like this?'

'That's good. Put a bit of elbow in it, dear, and it'll come up nicely. Now, what did you want to know?'

'You've owned the field a long time.'

'Since father died. That would be 1942. I was his only child — well, only surviving one. I gather I had a sister but I never knew her. So everything came to me when he passed away.'

'If you don't mind my asking, what constitutes "everything"?'

'Oh, not much. A couple of fields. The old mill. A few shops here and there.'

'And you were — what — twenty-seven? The boys must have been swarming round.'

'They were. But I saw through them, don't you worry! The ones who hadn't given me the time of day before didn't get the time of day from me after. There was one lad though. His father leased the mill, and he'd always had a soft spot for me.

He looked out for me when we were little. I'm under no illusions, I'm no beauty; never was. But he was a kind man.'

'What happened to him?'

'The Germans shot him. There was no reason. They rounded up half a dozen men and shot them as a reprisal.' The old lady paused in her polishing. 'I couldn't marry anyone else after that.' There was a moment of quiet before she resumed her buffing. 'Anyway, the riches didn't last long. The Communists grabbed it all. Mind, when they were turfed out I made sure I got as much back as I could. The priest, bless him — not Father Karel, the one before, Father Dominik — did all the paperwork for me. And I promised if I got it back I'd look after the church till I couldn't do it any longer. So here I am.'

'So who was renting the field?'

'Which one are we talking about? The one with the slope or the one by the stream?'

'Not the one with the stream. It slopes gently down to the road.'

'Ah, nobody told me that. Well, that one isn't rented to anyone at the moment. It used to be rented by a man who kept a bull there. He had two, you see, and it doesn't do to keep them in the same field when there are cows about. But he sold the bull at the spring market, so he didn't need the field this year.'

'And nobody else wanted it?'

'Times are hard around here. There's plenty who would have liked it, but they couldn't afford to pay for it, and I can't afford to give it away for nothing or nobody will pay their rents for the other fields. Anyway, it does it good to rest for a year now and then.'

'Do you ever go there?'

'It's a fair walk, dear. I doubt I've been past in the last ten years or so.'

Peiperová struggled to take this in. 'So if someone was camping in your field without your permission, you wouldn't know?'

'Not unless somebody told me. But the neighbours are good and they keep an eye open for that sort of thing.'

'Which particular neighbours would those be?'

'Did you see a house on the other side of the road about two hundred metres towards the village?'

'Yes.'

'Well, it isn't them. It's the ones next door.'

'Could I have their names?'

'Jeníček, Jiří and Lenka. Of course, when the bull was there we didn't have to worry too much about campers. And his droppings were great for the field.'

'I can imagine.'

'You're doing a good job there,' said Miss Valachová. 'Got time for another candlestick?'

'One more,' Peiperová replied, 'then I must get back to work.'

# Chapter 5

Slonský liked to be the first to arrive in the morning. It guaranteed him some peace and quiet, and allowed him to get some work done before he was interrupted by people wanting things from him.

This habit had been subjected to a degree of challenge in the past fifteen months by Navrátil, who thought it a clear duty to arrive when his boss did. Fortunately, he knew by now to speak only when spoken to for the first quarter of an hour or so. Peiperová was rarely late, but neither did she aim to be early.

It ought not to be thought that Slonský was a curmudgeon who disliked human interaction. He just wanted to determine how much of it there was and with whom it took place. It was not at all uncommon for him to loiter at the front desk for a while if Sergeant Mucha was on duty so that they could exchange gossip and gross calumnies about their colleagues.

Thus it was that Slonský was warned off a potential encounter.

'Doležal is looking for you,' Mucha muttered.

'Did he have a mallet and stake in his hands?'

'No. Actually, he seemed happy.'

'Happy? Doležal?'

'I know. It was creepy. Completely out of character.'

'Did he say where he was going to lie in wait?'

'He was going to his office. He said he'd try to catch you in yours.'

'I wonder what he wants.'

'You could try asking him,' suggested Mucha.

'Yes, but then I'd have to talk to him.'

'Isn't today his last day before he goes on loan to Pardubice?' Mucha asked.

'I suppose it will be.'

'Well, he probably wants to hand over any unfinished cases.'

'He shouldn't have any unfinished cases. He's not due there until Monday and he has a whole weekend before then.'

'He'll be packing up to move house.'

This took Slonský by surprise. The idea that people might need more than an afternoon to collect their worldly goods together was entirely novel and illustrated how little Slonský had allowed his life to be measured in possessions. This did not, however, indicate a zen-like clutter-free existence; Slonský's flat was simply furnished but irremediably untidy, or at least it had been until Věra had slipped back into his life with her manic obsession about washing plates between uses and laundering net curtains even when you didn't want to see out of the windows.

'Move house?'

'He can't commute to Pardubice every morning, can he? He'll have been lent a police flat for the duration.'

Holice was too small to warrant a criminal police presence of its own, so there was a small team at Pardubice which covered the region. Sedlák had been based there but had responsibility for a cluster of small towns and villages. Now Doležal would be part of the team temporarily — or, if Slonský could swing it, permanently.

'I hope it's a nice flat,' Slonský said. 'Maybe then he won't want to come back.'

'It's a temporary posting. He'd have to be persuaded to apply for the permanent one.'

'I'll work my charm on him. And if that doesn't work perhaps we can all move and not tell him where we've gone.'

'That would work,' agreed Mucha. 'It might stop all these members of the public strolling in and giving us work to do too.'

'I'm surprised we haven't thought of it before. Well, I can't stand here gabbing to you all day. I have subordinates upstairs to avoid.'

In this he failed dismally, because Doležal was sitting in front of his desk looking unreasonably content with life.

'Good morning!' he announced brightly.

'If you're going to be cheerful you can push off and annoy someone else,' Slonský replied.

'I just wanted to say I know you put a word in for me — Captain Lukas told me — and I'm very grateful.'

'Think nothing of it,' Slonský answered. 'As soon as I heard they needed a temporary lieutenant you came straight to mind.'

'I know you've already got the Holice enquiry under way,' replied Doležal, 'so I thought it might be convenient to brief me here before I go.'

'It's my case,' Slonský growled, exhibiting all the bonhomie of a bear whose friends have spotted that he has found a picnic basket.

'Of course. And it would be stupid for me to take it over on my first day when I'll have plenty of other things to learn. But I'll have to attend meetings with the Chief of Police at which he is bound to ask how it's going. Unless, of course, you'd rather attend those yourself?'

Doležal may be many things, thought Slonský, but he is not a fool.

'Of course,' said Slonský. 'Let's get comfortable. Navrátil, why don't you fetch us some coffees?'

'Decaffeinated for me,' declared Doležal. 'With low-fat milk.'
Slonský winced.

Some time later it crossed Slonský's mind that Peiperová was very late coming in to work.

'She's in Holice, sir,' explained Navrátil.

'What's she doing there?'

'You sent her, sir.'

'I sent her yesterday, Navrátil. It was a brief trip, not an extended holiday.'

'I don't think you'd go to Holice for a holiday, sir.'

'Perhaps not. Anyway, how come you know more about what she's doing than I do?'

'She rang last night to say she hadn't finished interviewing people so she was going to stay there and finish off today before she came back.'

'And she didn't think to clear her expenses with me first?'

'There aren't any, sir. One of the policewomen there said she could stay with her for the night. Said she'd be glad of the company.'

Slonský scratched his head. He could never imagine inviting anyone, even a policeman, into his home, and anyone who said they would like some company would be the very first person who should be avoided like the plague, he thought.

Peiperová was beginning to feel the same way. She had gratefully accepted the invitation from Officer Roubalová rather than drive back and forth to Prague, and after a quick trip to a small store to buy necessary toiletries, the two of them had headed for Roubalová's flat for a girls' night in, equipped with pasta, wine and chocolates.

Roubalová was a Sergeant who specialised in child and family matters, which was a slightly eccentric job choice for someone who was divorced and childless. To some extent those two things had gone together, because her brief marriage had led her to form some unshakeable views on love, families and men.

'Bastards,' she proclaimed, 'the whole lot of them. It's biological. They can't help it. They just have to spread their seed in as many places as possible.'

'Jan is very old-fashioned,' Peiperová explained. 'He's saving himself until we're married.'

'Good luck with that. Once he's found out about it you'll have to spike his coffee with bromide. Bastards.'

It was no better when Roubalová enquired if Peiperová hoped to have children.

'I don't know. I suppose so.'

'Little bastards. Swearing, underage drinking, breaking windows, they're all at it.'

'Surely not all of them?'

'All the ones I meet,' answered Roubalová, causing Peiperová to reflect that this was probably true. Whoever thought that all women had natural maternal gifts and that they would be a comfort to distressed women and children had failed to reckon with Roubalová, whose complete lack of sympathy for her fellow human beings briefly led Peiperová to regard Slonský as a beacon of empathetic feeling before she shook herself out of it.

They parted in the morning when a young male officer came to collect Roubalová so they could go across town to sort out a domestic dispute, at which the fresh-faced policeman would find himself comforting the crying woman while Roubalová jabbed her forefinger into the husband's diaphragm in the kitchen and threated to emasculate him with an ice-cream scoop she had spotted.

Jiří Jeníček was straightening one of the fence posts around his garden that had developed a slight lean when Peiperová drove up and greeted him.

'This must be about the explosion,' he said. 'There was a hell of a bang.'

'Did you go up to see what it was?'

'Not immediately. I had to check Lenka was all right first and I didn't know exactly where she was. In the end I found her in the bedroom. She had hidden beside the bed in case the Russians had come back.'

'The Russians?'

'You're too young to remember. They came through here in sixty-eight. And the old folks in the village remembered what they did in forty-five. No woman was safe. Every girl around here knows what to do if the Russians come. You grab the biggest knife you can find in the kitchen and hide somewhere in the house.'

'Why would she think the Russians were coming?'

'Well, who else would be setting off bombs here?'

Peiperová decided she had taken that line of questioning as far as it could go.

'So once you had found your wife…?'

'I walked up towards the field. I could see Captain Forman was by the gate. Of course, I didn't know that was where the noise had come from but I knew the general direction, so I headed off that way. I'm not as nimble as I used to be so it took me about five minutes, I suppose. But before I got there I could see there was something amiss, because the field gate was swinging open and it had been closed earlier.'

'You're sure of that?'

'If it's left open I get complaints from motorists. It's a big gate and it swings into the road so they have to swerve round it. I was going to shut it, but before I got there I was stopped by Captain Forman.'

'Did he say who called him?'

'No, just that he'd heard the noise and decided he ought to see what was going on.'

'And Captain Forman was at the gate?'

'Yes, he'd parked in the middle of the road outside my house and took out his gun. I could see it in his hand. He went into the field a few steps then came back to tell me I shouldn't go in there because it was so awful.'

'Did he say what had happened?'

'He said the metal detectors must have detonated a buried shell. But I can't understand that, because that field has been ploughed a few times to my knowledge and surely anything big enough to kill people would have been found before now?'

'Did you know the metal detectors were going to be checking out the field?'

'No, they didn't ask me. So far as I know they didn't ask Irina either.'

'Miss Valachová confirms that she didn't know.'

'Well, there you are then. Mind, I'm surprised at Sedlák. He was usually very fussy about rights of way and getting permission.'

Peiperová paused to reflect. 'Do you know where the metal detectors had been exploring before this week?'

Jeníček removed his cap to scratch his head, as if this might somehow aid his memory. 'They were in the wood at the end of the lane the other week.'

'Where's that?'

Jeníček walked her to the gate. 'If you go down past Irina's field and bear round to the left there's a footpath into the woods. The highway is quite recent but for centuries there was a path that we used to get to the high road to Pardubice. Procházka had an idea that there might be stuff worth finding along that path because it been used for so long.'

'That's about a hundred and fifty metres further away than the field?' Peiperová estimated.

'About that. That's where they've been working. I don't know that they'd found anything there.'

'But if they've been doing it for a while they must have thought it was worth the effort.'

'Ah, you don't know these types! They're fanatics in their own way. They think nothing of spending a weekend dismantling a manure heap if they think there might be something underneath it. And there usually isn't, but it doesn't put them off trying again next weekend.'

Peiperová thanked him and returned to the car. There were questions she would like to ask Captain Forman, but she thought that perhaps they ought to come from Slonský rather than her.

Slonský was very willing to use the technical services that police scientists could provide. It was his private opinion that many of the technicians were very lucky that they had found gainful employment given their multiple and flagrant personality issues, but he never doubted their technical skills or their usefulness to him.

It was the scientists elsewhere that he found difficult. Experts of every kind perplexed him because he had never had the kind of enquiring mind that wants to know everything about a subject. Slonský was capable of understanding a great many things, but as soon as he had used the information, he forgot it. There was no point in cluttering up your memory with stuff you were never going to need again. At a pinch he could probably remember the years when Slavia had won the Czech hockey championship, and he had a pretty sound grasp of brewing practices good and bad, but otherwise he liked to keep the mental decks clear.

As an example of how this accumulation of knowledge could all go horribly wrong, he needed to look no further than one of the boys he had known at school, who had gone on to earn a Ph.D. in medieval history and knew everything there was to know about plagues and pestilences except, of course, how to treat them or anything else that Slonský would have considered useful knowledge. Still, it was good to know that if he ever caught the Black Death he knew someone who could tell him ten or twelve cures that definitely would not work.

Kohoutek, on the other hand, seemed relatively normal, or as near to it as anyone to whom Valentin had ever introduced him. His enjoyment of a beer or two elevated him in Slonský's estimation, to the point where Slonský had taken his telephone number in case something else turned up where his expertise might be helpful. And now an idea was beginning to form in his head for which Kohoutek might come in handy — but first he needed to pay someone a visit. And he needed to go on his own, so he had to find something else for Navrátil and Peiperová to do while he did it.

The Security Information Service of the Czech Republic was widely viewed by serving police officers as about as useful as a chocolate coffee pot. BIS, to give it its Czech acronym, had no police powers and therefore could not arrest anybody, so if they wanted someone detained they had to ask the police to do it, but often they would not tell you why. Of course, before the Wall came down, arresting somebody and refusing to tell them what they were being charged with was normal practice, but now it was generally frowned upon, and most police officers felt uncomfortable with telling someone that they were being arrested but they did not know what it was all about.

BIS occupied an eight-storey office block in Stodůlky, so there must have been plenty of them in there, but trying to get an appointment was still a challenge. Slonský suspected that they might have been working on the puffer fish principle, making themselves look big so others would not give them a hard time. If so, it wasn't working — or at least it was not going to work this afternoon.

He had deputed Peiperová to trawl such army records as she could find to see if they could work out who, if anyone, might have been the men detached into the Ghost Battery. He was fairly sure that it would be fruitless because those who selected them would have been in a position to conceal their existence by losing any relevant papers, but it had to be done for form's sake, and it would keep her out of the way while he was asking a few questions on an unofficial basis. Navrátil, meanwhile, was engaged in a similar search of police records for anyone who had been shopped to the police as a potentially subversive or treasonous entity in the Pardubice region. Navrátil had already discovered that the locals there must have been of a deeply suspicious nature, since they had complained about a Jehovah's Witness, two people who were "cycling suspiciously" and the organisers of a triathlon in the last six months alone.

Contacts between the police and BIS were strictly regulated to ensure that the two of them did not collaborate to stage a coup. Slonský felt this was unnecessary since, if he had wanted to stage a coup with any prospect of success, the last people he would have involved were BIS. But he might have made an exception for Milan Poznar.

Poznar had worked with Slonský once before on a case involving a man who was smuggling industrial secrets out of an engineering company. This would not normally have attracted the attention of BIS, except that the company held a contract for armament development, and there was some concern that those secrets might be at risk too. Poznar had been sceptical that anyone had been attempting to steal those secrets, and Slonský had proved him right when it turned out that the thief had actually wanted the laptop, not the information carelessly left on it, though not before some overzealous BIS officers had attempted to persuade him to confess with the help of a flight of stairs and a lump of wood. Over a beer afterwards, which stretched into several beers, a sausage or two and a very uncomfortable night on Poznar's couch, the two had bemoaned the difficulty of getting their organisations to work together in any rational way and had cooked up a more informal method of contact.

Slonský knew that all phone calls to Stodůlky were recorded and that officers were not supposed to receive work calls on their mobile phones, but he also knew that they turned them to silent rather than switching them off. Thus, he left a voicemail on Poznar's cellphone inviting him to a sausage at a nearby café at 14:00.

Precisely at the appointed hour the café door opened and Poznar walked in, carefully scanning the room for anyone he knew. Slonský was sitting behind a pillar on the right hand side.

'Good choice,' Poznar muttered. 'Don't want to be seen from the street.'

'You work with some very suspicious people,' Slonský remarked. 'There's not a lot of trust within our security services.'

'Nor in our police. You could have asked me to come to your office.'

'I'm a natural plotter. I don't see why I should tell anyone anything they don't need to know. Coffee or something stronger?'

They ordered their drinks. Despite Slonský's exhortations Poznar declined any food, citing the need to keep in shape.

'I need to keep in shape too,' said Slonský. 'It's just a different shape.'

'I heard a rumour you were trying to lose twenty kilos,' Poznar replied.

'Who told you that?' a shocked Slonský gasped.

'We're the security service. It's our job to know everything. In this case, it's the talk of the police gym.'

'Ah. I've been shopped by Čada.'

'Not that I know of. It was more the result of the bitter disappointment felt by some who had lost heavily on the sweepstake about whether you would pass your captain's medical.'

'People bet on that?' Slonský asked.

'You know our colleagues. They'll bet on anything. I'm told you could get three to one against your passing.'

'Passing the medical or passing away?'

'Passing the medical. Actual death was pretty long odds. Twenty to one at the very least.'

'Well, that's reassuring.'

'There weren't many takers.'

'Many? There shouldn't have been any!'

'Don't get me wrong. They didn't want it to happen. They just thought that if they pocketed a small fortune at least some good would have come of your passing.'

'I don't know what to say.'

'Your desk sergeant did all right.'

'Mucha?'

'Took quite a plunge on your passing the medical and cleaned up, I hear. Though he had inside information from that woman of yours.'

'My wife?'

'No, the young officer. She was convinced you would do it.'

Slonský filed the information away with a view to getting at least ten per cent off Mucha when he next saw him. 'To business. I need to know something but I have a little information to offer.'

'I'm intrigued,' Poznar replied. 'People giving us information before we've threatened violence is a fairly unusual experience for me.'

'It's about the explosion at Holice.'

'The shell from World War II? Well, obviously that's bunkum. So what have you discovered?' Poznar asked.

'It looks as if the four men were tied up, placed in a circle and then someone threw a grenade into the middle of them.'

'Ouch. Doesn't sound like an accident, does it?'

'It sounds like somebody with a big secret to keep to me,' Slonský suggested.

'I can see why you might think that. But there's obviously a security angle which isn't clear to me yet.'

'Hold your horses. I'm coming to that. I've spoken to a fellow called Kohoutek. Works for a think tank.'

'I know him.'

'He told me the story of the Ghost Battery.'

'That old chestnut.'

'Yes, and he didn't believe it either, until now.' Slonský fished in his pocket for the photograph of the tracks in the field which he handed over without a word.

Poznar inspected it and let loose a low whistle. 'This is the field where the killings took place?'

'The very same.'

'And presumably forensics are telling you that whatever made these tracks was in the field when the murders took place?'

'Yes, they are. So my first thought was to ask you whether you know of any organisation that could hide a gun for forty years and what they're keeping hold of it for.'

Poznar passed the photograph back. 'I'd better not keep that or I'll have to log it and you'll have us all over your back. We'll have to see it at some time but I'm sure you can arrange not to know about the gun for a few days.'

'I'm an expert at not knowing stuff. I can avoid knowing things for months on end in the right circumstances.'

Poznar pinched his nose as he thought. 'There's a group called New Bohemia. Right wing, get rid of immigrants, usher in a new age of aggressive national assertiveness. But I doubt they would be involved in this.'

'Why not?'

'They're a gang of nutters. They're much more interested in pamphlets and speeches than direct action. They were also only formed about eight years ago, so how would they get a gun from 1968?'

'Any others?' Slonský asked.

'Plenty, but this is a step up for any of them, and it's concerning that they've had this weaponry for forty years without our knowing about it.'

'A gun is a big thing to have up your sleeve, but you can't stage a coup with one gun and a box of grenades. They must have more.'

'Or they're unrealistic fantasists. But maybe they don't plan a coup as such.'

'Meaning?'

'This sounds like a starting gun,' Poznar suggested. 'In itself, it has largely symbolic significance, but they can use it to send a message to sympathisers to rise up and join them.'

'Is that likely?'

'I don't think so, but these types are very good at deluding themselves that it only needs a spark to set the country ablaze. It's the philosophy of Our Home, for example.'

'Our Home?'

'They take their name from the national anthem "Where is my home?". I think of them because their newsletter is called The Spark.'

'Are they a significant threat?'

'I'd have said not. But that was before I knew they might have a gun. Where is it now, by the way?'

'I don't know,' Slonský replied. 'We tracked it leaving the village and heading for the highway, but where it went after that is anyone's guess.'

'It would attract some attention on the road, surely?'

'Not necessarily. Think how often we see military vehicles moving around the country. A squadron of tanks would be noticed, but I'm not sure one vehicle on its own would. And they may have moved it when the road was quiet. Against that, if the explosion was at six it would have been daylight. I'm reluctant to put out a public message in case it alerts them to the fact that we know about the gun and they decide to get on and use it. I've got the traffic police looking out for it from a helicopter, but it's a camouflaged vehicle. Its makers designed it not to be seen.'

'I'll see what's come in recently about Our Home or other subversive activity in the Pardubice region,' Poznar suggested.

'That would be helpful. Now, to the important stuff. Are your beloved Sparta going to win the football league again this year?'

The traffic police had not seen the gun, but a sharp-eyed pilot had spotted some damage to a verge that he thought might have been done by a large vehicle, so Slonský rang Peiperova and told her to take a look on her way back to Prague. She rang him back within the hour.

'It's just the other side of the highway to Holice, sir.'

'I know where it is, Peiperová. I sent you there, remember?'

'Yes, sir. Sorry, sir. There are tracks on the verge like we saw before, and a substantial tree on the bend has been taken out by whatever passed.'

'Okay. Let's assume it went that way. Are you in a marked car?'

'No, sir, plain blue.'

'Not in uniform?'

'No, sir.'

'Good. It's safer that way. Take a look around and see if you can pin down where it went. But be careful. Don't get out of the car and don't go unusually slowly. Wherever they've put it, let's assume that someone is watching in case outsiders take an interest. And remember that if they've killed four people including the local police lieutenant, they're not going to lose sleep over anything that happens to you.'

'No, sir.'

'I'm not talking anything exhaustive, Peiperová. No more than a couple of hours on it.'

'Understood, sir.'

Slonský rang off and sat for a few moments staring at his phone, then decided to ring Navrátil.

'I just wanted you to know what Peiperová is doing, lad. She's following a sighting of the damage done by the gun moving after the explosion. I've told her to stay in the car but have a drive around for a couple of hours looking for any more damage, then come back. If she doesn't appear by, say, seven o'clock I want to know. If I don't hear I'll assume everything is okay.'

'I'll call her in a while to check everything is in order, sir.'

'You do that, Navrátil. I don't have any reason to think she's in special danger but we just don't know what we're up against.'

When Slonský filled Captain Lukas in he was extremely concerned.

'I'm extremely concerned,' Lukas said. 'Extremely concerned indeed.'

'So am I, sir. Most of these groups seem to be pretty inept but this one seems to be more ruthless than most. My security contact pointed the finger at an outfit called Our Home, but he said there could be plenty of others.'

Lukas tutted. He was an international class tutter, but then he had plenty of practice, especially when talking to Slonský. 'I've never heard of them. Have you?'

'No, sir.'

'Josef, you're an Acting Captain now. You don't have to call me "sir" any more.'

'I haven't got the official bit of paper in my hand yet, sir. I'll believe it when that happens.'

'I've been thinking. Perhaps it's worth having a little word with Sergeant Fulnek.'

'Fulnek? But he's in organised crime.'

'Yes, but I'm sure you've heard him holding forth with some unsavoury views from time to time. He may have an opinion about these Our Home fellows.'

'He may, but it could be an admiring one.'

In fact, Fulnek was quite balanced in his opinion. On the one hand, he thought that Our Home was a romantic association of intellectuals with no practical aptitude whatsoever who talked a good game but had done nothing concrete to reassert Czech nationhood. On the other hand, he thought that they would never spot someone trying to infiltrate them so it was possible that things might be done in their name without their active participation.

Slonský found it difficult to conceal his distaste for Fulnek's brand of nationalism, so he did not bother to try.

'There's nothing wrong with being patriotic, sir,' the young sergeant maintained. 'But I wouldn't countenance anything illegal.'

'I believe you,' said Slonský, 'because you're not stupid and you'll know how hard a court would come down on you if you did.'

'Never mind a court,' Fulnek answered wistfully. 'You haven't met my mother.'

Peiperová returned around half past six and presented herself in the shared office where Navrátil and Slonský were waiting for her.

'What did you find, Peiperová?'

'No sign of the gun, sir, as such. The tree on the bend had been hit pretty hard though. I think the driver couldn't get round in one and hit it as he reversed back to get a better angle on the turn.'

'Don't be sexist, young lady. The driver could be a woman for all we know. In fact, since they hit a tree … well, never mind. Let's leave that one open.'

'Yes, sir,' Peiperová responded through gritted teeth. By common consent she was the best driver of the three people in the room, which was unsurprising given that she had much more practice than the others. Whichever combination of officers went out, she was more likely than not to be handed the keys.

'There's something else, isn't there? Out with it.'

Peiperová appeared hesitant as if unconvinced by her own intuition, but she walked over to the large map of the Czech Republic on the wall. 'It's just this, sir. This is the road the gun passed along. The tree is just here, as the road turns slightly north-east. But about three kilometres further on the road turns sharp left to resume its northward course and there's a small hump-backed bridge over the river here. It's very narrow but there's no sign that anything scraped the side.'

'So you think it turned off before that?'

'I can't see any alternative, sir. But there are no roads. There is a track and a farm entrance to the right and a large yard to the left.'

'Meaning that you think the gun may be in one of those places?'

'We'd have to look for tracks, sir, but it seems so.'

'Good work, Peiperová. We'll get a party together and give it a look over tomorrow.'

'Sir, won't it be dangerous?' asked Navrátil.

'It certainly will,' agreed Slonský. 'That's why we'll take an armed assault team. And if you happen to be passing a church tonight, lad, you might say an extra prayer for us.'

'You could do it yourself, sir,' Navrátil responded.

'I could, but you're the one who has kept his membership up. Go and enjoy some sort of movie, young people. I'll get everything set up for tomorrow. Peiperová, I don't think tomorrow will be a day for wearing a skirt.'

'No, sir.'

'You either, Navrátil,' Slonský added, having remembered what he was told in the gender neutrality training classes.

# Chapter 6

When Slonský made his arrangements with the tactical weapons unit he was a little surprised at the meeting place that they nominated, and even more taken aback when he arrived to find two helicopters waiting.

'Much quicker than cars,' explained the unit's commander, who wore a waistcoat filled with so many gadgets and attachments that it was doubtful whether he could right himself if he fell over. To Slonský's delight he noted that the commander's flak jacket and helmet were clearly marked with his rank, meaning that he would be the first one targeted by the villains and there was every chance that other key officers present, namely himself, would be able to get themselves flat on the ground or into a ditch and keep safe.

'If you'd just put these on,' the commander ordered, handing each of them a flak jacket and helmet, 'we'll take off. Strictly I should split you between the helicopters. Who's second in command?'

Slonský hated those questions. Navrátil had been in the post longer, but Peiperová had joined the police earlier, having signed up straight from school whereas Navrátil had taken a law degree before joining the police academy as an officer cadet.

'I'll go in one and these two can go in the other,' he announced. 'It'll give them something to talk about on the way there.'

Peiperová took everything in her stride. Navrátil, though admirable in many ways, was not a great aficionado of air travel. A plane was one thing, but a helicopter was something else. For a start, Navrátil understood the physics of winged flight. He had never quite worked out how a helicopter stayed in the air, and the fact that the side door was open caused him a great deal of worry and led to his checking the shackle that kept him secured in his seat roughly every thirty seconds.

The deputy commander winked at him from the other side of the helicopter. 'Your first time?' he asked.

'First time in a police helicopter,' Navrátil agreed, leaving open the matter of any civilian flight (of which there had been none, but he preferred to maintain some mystery around that).

If two police helicopters were an unusual sight in the countryside around Prague the locals on the ground seemed to be doing a very good job of minding their own business, thought Slonský, who was watching for any sign of untoward energy down below as they flew over. The helicopters swooped down late to conceal their landing site as long as possible and made contact in a riverside meadow a little under a kilometre from the farm that Peiperová had identified.

With all the occupants decanted the pilots switched off their engines and alighted to stand guard in case anyone felt like adding a couple of choppers to their target. Meanwhile the police trotted through the fields in single file, a dozen sleek figures in black, two fit officers in mufti with black flak jackets and one well-built specimen who was wishing that he had brought a bicycle. However, a little reflection brought Slonský to realise that the weight he had lost had made quite a difference to his ability to run, and he had no doubt that if shooting started it would inspire him to even greater efforts. It always had in the past.

The commander held up his hand to order them to stop, then produced a baffling series of hand signals which clearly conveyed plenty to his team but left Slonský desperately trying to recall what he had been taught years before. He was fairly sure that one of the signals meant "I am about to slow down and turn right" and he was inclined to think another showed that someone had hit a puck the length of the ice rink, but in the end he decided to follow Navrátil who seemed to be confident that he knew what was being indicated and had peeled off to the left with half a dozen of the armed team. Slonský checked that his own weapon was in his hand, loaded, but with the safety catch engaged. He noted with satisfaction that Peiperová had attached herself to the other half of the party, though he dimly recalled that her scores on the range were consistently better than Navrátil's. Navrátil attributed this to her longer arms which meant that she was ten centimetres nearer the target when she fired.

On a signal from the commander the men hurdled the low wooden fence and fanned out around the farmyard, checking all the outbuildings in turn. They met no resistance and might have left as quietly as they came had they not encountered a farmhand who emerged from the outside privy still adjusting his clothing and jerked his hands high as he saw the guns levelled at him. This was wise given the firepower on display, but less satisfactory when his trousers slowly descended to his knees and his panicky face pleaded for permission to pull them up since he could see a lady present. Peiperová turned her face away.

'Slowly pull them up,' ordered the commander, 'but keep your hands where we can see them.'

'I will, I will!' came the response.

Having restored his trousers to a decent height, the man pointed his hands to the sky once more.

'Police!' snapped the commander, which seemed unnecessary to Slonský given that it was written on all their chests and backs. 'Name?'

'Smec, Marek.'

'Who else is here?'

'Just me and the old couple who own the farm.'

'Are they in the house?'

'Yes. The old man can't get out now. Bad chest.'

Slonský decided it was time to ease the tension a little. 'If your men can search the farm, we'll question the three people. Peiperová, you take the woman. Navrátil, Mr Smec is yours. I'll speak to the old man.'

'Do you want us to check out the house?' asked the commander.

'I'm armed,' said Slonský. 'We'll be fine. If you hear shooting it'll probably mean I've dropped my gun.'

He strode into the house followed by Peiperová. They found the old woman in the kitchen making soup. Although alarmed at their appearance, she agreed to sit and be questioned, provided Peiperová stirred the soup at intervals.

Slonský mounted the stairs and found the farmer sitting in an old armchair by the window, which was slightly open. He wore his pyjamas with a pullover on top.

'I heard what you said down there. Why do you need all those guns? Are there bandits about?' he asked.

'I hope not. We're on the lookout for an old army vehicle,' Slonský told him.

'Thought you might be,' came the reply. 'I saw it come up the road on Liberation Day. I thought there must have been a parade somewhere.'

Slonský could have slapped himself. That was why nobody had noticed it. They expected military vehicles to be moving around on Liberation Day.

'Just one vehicle though?'

'Yes, just the one. Some sort of artillery thing, self-propelled gun if I'm any judge, though my military service was a long time ago.'

'Excellent. That's what we're looking for. Did you see where it went?'

'Not really. I can only see part of the road from here. Mind, whoever was driving it was useless. He got stuck on the corner and reversed over a tree trying to get round. And he would never have got it over the stone bridge up the road.' The old man swallowed some air and had a cough before continuing. 'I didn't see it again, but I think I heard it.'

'What time did it go past?'

'Going up the road, probably between six and seven. But it was nearly dark by the time it came back down.'

'It turned around?'

'Must have done. As I say, he'd have demolished that old bridge if he'd tried to get something that size across it. I reckon he must have reversed back to the old coal yard and turned round in there so he could go forward down the hill again. But I was having my supper then. My wife could tell you the time.'

Slonský thanked him and returned to the kitchen.

'Then you add a sprig of rosemary just for the scent,' the old lady was explaining.

Peiperová lifted the spoon from the pot and dipped her little finger in the soup. 'Very nice,' she said.

'Forgive my intrusion,' Slonský interrupted, 'but I wondered if any crime was being solved today?'

'Sorry, sir. We'd finished the questioning. Mrs Hejdová didn't see the gun but she says her husband saw it and they both heard it while they were having supper just after eight o'clock.'

'I know the time because I listened to the news headlines on the wireless before I took it up on the tray,' the woman added. 'We eat together at supper, you see.'

'Very nice, I'm sure. It'll be a bit of company. And does Marek eat with you?'

'No, he finishes about six and goes home. He has a wife and a lovely little girl in the village. But it was Liberation Day so he'd only have come up for the milking.'

'Do many people walk up and down that road?'

'Not these days. Since they built the highway there's no need.'

Smec told Navrátil that he came up at five to do the afternoon milking and was gone by about half-past six. He did not see the gun but he heard a loud rumbling noise while he was in the milking shed.

'That makes sense,' Slonský said as the three detectives compared notes. 'If you're going to kill all the witnesses you'd get the gun on its way before you throw the grenade, otherwise you're attracting curious locals to run towards the very thing you're trying to hide.'

The commander returned to confirm that there were no signs that any large vehicle had been on the farm. Rather than move the helicopters again he had sent eight men to inspect the coal yard. They reported that the gun was not there but there were track marks in the coal dust that still littered the place.

'Well, it's not here,' said Slonský, 'and there's nowhere it could be hiding at the side of the road, so we conclude they took it back to the highway to move it somewhere else under cover of darkness.'

'Perhaps they needed to get a new hiding place ready, sir,' suggested Peiperová.

'I don't want to disparage local colleagues,' Slonský replied, knowing he was about to do just that, 'but what on earth are they doing while folks are driving artillery around a small town? Isn't there anyone on duty in the evenings? Things have changed since I was a lad. Back then you couldn't pump your bicycle tyres up without the whole street knowing about it. Now you can pretty well set up a military coup and nobody bothers to mention it.'

'Do you want a lift back to Prague?' asked the commander.

'I was taking it for granted,' snapped Slonský. 'It's a hell of a walk.'


Later, joining Valentin in their usual place, Slonský looked wistfully at a plate of sausages on the next table.

'I'm convinced this diet is causing my brain to shrink,' he opined.

'Only if you had a fat brain before,' Valentin replied.

'I just have a feeling that there is something big behind all this stuff with the gun, but it seems so improbable. The security service doesn't know of any impending threat, the local police are as much use as paper underwear and there isn't any sign of other thefts. But if they don't intend to use the gun, why kill to conceal its existence?'

'I'm amazed you haven't found the gun. I mean, it's not small, is it?'

'That's a statement of the obvious if ever there was one. They must have found somewhere else to hide it.'

'Perhaps it's back where it's been for the past thirty-nine years?'

'Then why move it at all in the first place? Were they planning a coup for Liberation Day that didn't come off? There's no sign of that. And, being Liberation Day, people don't seem to have paid any attention to large military vehicles rolling round the country. If we put out a public appeal for sightings we'd be swamped with people telling us about jeeps and minibuses.'

'So what do you do now?'

'I'm waiting for the technical report on the grenade fragments. Just maybe there'll be something in there to give us a lead. Doležal is getting to know the area and maybe he'll sniff something out.'

'I thought you were looking forward to getting rid of him.'

'I was. I am. But he's not that bad a detective. It's as a human being that he's a failure. Teetotaller. What more need I say?'

'I suppose I'm five-sevenths of a teetotaller now.'

Slonský shuddered. 'The world is going mad,' he said. 'Completely barking mad.'

Returning to his office Slonský found himself confronted with another problem, albeit one he might have anticipated, though this one wore a lot of black and tried to avoid notice as far as was possible.

Just as Slonský had Navrátil to fetch him coffee, applaud his brilliant deductions and do the donkey-work, so Doležal had Rada. Rada was a year older than Navrátil and had graduated in the previous academy intake, and the two of them got on about as well as a pair of bulls in a field full of cows. Slonský knew very little about Rada, but the fact that he was able to provoke Navrátil to uncharitable thoughts fed his concern about the prospect of them working together, because Slonský had found it difficult to irritate his young assistant and had been obliged to up his game considerably before he found a way of doing it. Now, of course, it was much easier. He had only to suggest that Peiperová was developing acne or that she was putting a bit of weight on her midriff to ensure a silent hour or two, but for a long time he was nonplussed by Navrátil's tolerance and self-discipline.

Rada was sitting on the corner of Navrátil's desk making small talk when Slonský entered the room. It took barely a moment to divine from Navrátil's deep frown that he was struggling to maintain his poise in the face of Rada's incessant provocation, which, in this case, consisted mainly of continuing to breathe. Time to intervene, thought Slonský, before Navrátil bites the end off his pencil.

'Rada! What brings you here?'

'Lieutenant Doležal said I'd be reporting to you while he is on secondment to Pardubice, sir.'

'Did he? I thought he'd given you some work to get on with.'

'He did, but I've done it, sir. I wanted to know what you'd like me to do now.'

Navrátil could have answered that one, Slonský thought, but decided it would be improper to invite him to do so. 'Has anything come in while I was out of the office?' Slonský asked.

'I've already asked, sir,' said Rada.

'Is there anything you need to hand over, Navrátil?'

'No, sir. I'm on top of everything.'

'Sit down here, Rada, before Navrátil's desk develops a slope. I have to admit I thought Lieutenant Doležal might need you in his new role.'

'There's already a full complement of officers at Pardubice, sir. The only vacancy was the one created by the death of Lieutenant Sedlák.'

'I see.'

'I realise, of course, that this will all be sorted out in a couple of weeks when Officer Peiperová goes on secondment and there'll be a vacancy in your team…'

At this point there was a loud snap as Navrátil broke his pencil. Rada and Slonský instinctively turned to see what the noise was.

'I'll… I'll just get a new … pencil,' Navrátil stuttered.

'Why don't you have your coffee break now?' Slonský suggested amiably, 'then you can bring one back for me when you've finished. Rada and I will have a little chat about his future while you're gone.'

Navrátil was not at all certain that he wanted to be out of the room while such a conversation was taking place, but the set of Slonský's jaw inhibited any discussion on the matter, so he nodded mutely.

'There's a pencil here,' Rada announced, picking up a stub from Slonský's desk, which Slonský quickly collared.

'That's my pencil,' Slonský grumbled. 'Navrátil is fussy about his pencils, aren't you, lad? You'll want a new, unchewed one.'

'Yes, sir.'

'Well, run along, Navrátil. Rada and I need a bit of privacy.'

It must be admitted that in the normal run of things Slonský was not known for his sensitivity to the feelings of others. Peiperová had been pleasantly surprised by his modern attitude to women's equality, but this was largely based on his hatred of domestic violence, a general feeling that women should be placed on a pedestal and a strong belief that anyone who liked hanging around their home all day was deeply to be pitied, which was entirely understandable where his own flat was concerned. Until his wife Věra came round with a mop he had completely forgotten that the linoleum in his kitchen was supposed to be sky blue.

At this moment he was trying to see things from Navrátil's point of view, and he did not like what he saw. Navrátil had completed fifteen months under Slonský's tutelage and, while two years was the normal span for a mentoring post, if he wanted to go elsewhere it would be very hard for Slonský to stop him, short of outright perjury in his appraisal documents. And the continued presence of Navrátil at the desk at right angles to his own was the best lure he possessed to drag Peiperová back after her year with the Director of Criminal Police, when the world would be her oyster and she would, presumably, have become hot property within the police force. Admittedly it had not worked that way for her predecessor Kuchař, but then he was a complex mixture of senior politician's son and empty skull which had taxed the Director considerably until he hit on the idea of recommending him for a posting to Europol, whither he was bound at the end of the month.

Slonský's master plan was simple. He would pull the strings, Navrátil and Peiperová would deliver the goods, and he would keep Lieutenant Dvorník on hand in case of any rough stuff. Dvorník was not, perhaps, the most intellectually gifted member of the team of detectives, but he was a keen hunter and possessed a weapons cabinet that would have been the envy of several small nations. Dvorník was assisted by young Hauzer, otherwise known as The Invisible Policeman, who was unobjectionable and kept the department informed of any pending additions to Dvorník's family, currently standing at eight children but rumoured to be aiming for double figures before he finished. Dvorník and his wife had each been married before and they had custody of all the consequent children, though people were not quite sure which offspring belonged to which relationship. It was claimed that Dvorník himself had it written in the back of his diary in case he forgot.

Add to that Slonský's plan to encourage Doležal to find a post somewhere else, and the future had looked rosy from Slonský's point of view, but now Rada had turned up and lobbed a considerable spanner in the works. Slonský could hardly sack someone he barely knew, particularly because it would leave the department under strength, but neither did he want his beautiful project disrupted. The only option was to persuade Rada to apply for a job elsewhere.

'We should get to know each other a little better,' Slonský began, using the tone of voice of a benevolent uncle.

'Sir?'

'I mean in the professional sense.'

'Oh, right, good.'

'Tell me, lad, where do you see your future lying? What would you like to be when you grow — when you have a bit more service under your belt?'

'I'm happy here, sir.'

'You are?'

'I like crime, sir. And you get a good mix of it here. Robbery, murder, you name it, we get it.'

It crossed Slonský's mind that Klinger in the fraud squad upstairs was always trying to tempt Navrátil away from him. 'Have you ever thought of a career in fraud?'

'Fraud, sir?'

'Pitting your wits against the criminal, using your meticulous turn of mind to discover what he has been up to…'

'I'm no good at maths, sir.'

'I'm not sure that's as big a barrier in the fraud squad as you might think,' Slonský suggested, but he had to admit that he wasn't really convincing himself. Klinger's one-time deputy would soon be released from prison but even an optimist like Slonský had to confess that the chances that he would be re-employed by the fraud squad given that he had been convicted of fraud himself would be fairly slim.

Candidates who wanted to fill the gaps in the fraud squad had to submit to an interview by Klinger which, in Slonský's opinion, was where the problem lay. Having once met their potential new boss, many of them saw to it that they flunked the interview, finding his little habits to be a deterrent. Klinger only ever touched door handles with a handkerchief, and his compulsion to align the edges of folders, lay out his pens in a perfectly parallel arrangement and drink coffee only from his personal crockery led some to feel that they would struggle to provide satisfaction. Add to this the fact that he was a fluent German speaker and was often to be seen with a large hardback book with an impenetrable title in his hands, and the desirability of a career in fraud flickered and died in many breasts.

'All I'm saying, Rada, is don't rule it out. Klinger must be retiring in a few years and there will be relatively few candidates with the necessary experience to replace him.'

The flaw in this argument was that Klinger was younger than Slonský, who would therefore retire first, but fortunately Rada was too fixated on denying any interest in fraud to concentrate on that issue.

'I'd rather stay here, sir. I think I could learn a lot from you.'

If Captain Lukas had heard that he would have cringed, thought Slonský, whose face was then illuminated by a happy thought.

'Of course, Lieutenant Doležal is jumping the gun a bit,' Slonský asserted. 'Captain Lukas is still in charge here for the next month and a bit. I couldn't possibly make any decisions without consulting him. I'll tell you what, lad. Why don't you take a good look at the professional development courses we run? This may be an opportunity for you to get some training in your portfolio while the good lieutenant is doing his own thing in Pardubice. Then you'd be equipped to be even more use to him when he comes back.'

'He is coming back, then, sir?'

'Oh, yes! Probably. Can you see Lieutenant Doležal being happy in a backwater like Pardubice?' Slonský crossed his fingers under the desk. One can but hope, he thought.

Everyone needs someone in whom they can confide. Slonský would not have admitted it, but for him this role was supplied by Sergeant Mucha. They had joined the police at around the same time, but Mucha had missed out on promotion to lieutenant the first time he tried and had never wanted to face that disappointment again; besides which, he enjoyed work on the front desk. You never knew what was going to face you across that counter.

At this moment, what faced him was a perplexed Slonský. An old friend like Mucha could tell he was troubled because he had removed his hat so he could think better.

'Quite a conundrum you've got there,' Mucha opined after Slonský had described his interview with Rada.

'Lukas must have put up with this for years,' Slonský whined.

'Well, from you, certainly,' agreed Mucha.

'I almost feel guilty now about some of the stuff I dumped on him. Almost.'

'So let's get this straight. If Rada joins your team when Peiperová goes, you think Navrátil will have a hissy fit and pack his bags.'

'I don't think. I know. There's something about Rada that gets right up Navrátil's nose and turns him from a fluffy bunny into a psychotic rabbit. I've no idea what it is, but it's there.'

'There you are, then. The first step is to find out what it is. But if he hasn't volunteered it, it's probably something that he doesn't find easy to talk about, so you'll have to be tactful and sensitive.'

'I can do that,' Slonský responded. 'Tactful is my middle name.'

On the way up the stairs Slonský decided that the most tactful way to approach this with Navrátil was not to talk to him at all. There was an alternative way to discover Navrátil's innermost thoughts, so he made a quick phone call and fixed an appointment for around twenty minutes later in the café on the corner. This was a favourite meeting place though it suffered from the considerable drawback of being full of police much of the time, many of whom Slonský did not want to speak to, but it caused him to reflect that it should not surprise him that there was one colleague whom Navrátil disliked given that he himself despised around a third of the police he had ever met.

It dawned upon Slonský that he had not eaten for a while, so he ordered a pastry with his coffee and listlessly picked at it while he waited for his informant to arrive. How often had he done this during his career! Sitting in grubby cafés with a coffee watching the clock tick by, reading yesterday's newspaper and trying to avoid being recognised. At least on this occasion he wasn't going to have to pay for information.

Peiperová entered and sat opposite him.

'Sir, you haven't lapsed, have you?'

'Lapsed?'

She pointed at his pastry.

'It's lunch. I haven't had time to eat. It's the heavy responsibilities of my job, Peiperová.'

'I thought you were having lunch with Valentin, sir?'

'It was a liquid lunch. A non-alcoholic liquid lunch,' he added mournfully.

Slonský was touched to see the obvious concern on Peiperová's face.

'I hope you're not becoming anorexic, sir.'

Never in his entire life had Slonský anticipated hearing those words. At the age of four he had been told by the nurse at the polyclinic that he must eat less or he would grow up fat and that warning had been repeated with varying degrees of intensity over the succeeding fifty-five years, but never, ever, had anyone expressed a concern that he might not be eating enough. He was quite touched.

'Just exercising iron self-control, Peiperová. Pure, unadulterated willpower.'

'I'm impressed, sir. I don't think I could do what you're doing.'

'I don't think you'll ever need to, lass. You've got good genes. I, on the other hand, inherited a propensity to the fuller figure. Not quite on the scale of my Aunt Eva, admittedly, but we Slonskýs incline towards being well covered.'

Slonský had been very attached to his Aunt Eva, of blessed memory, a woman who closely resembled a ninety kilogram onion in appearance but whose strudel would have delighted the angels. She might have lived longer if she had left them bigger portions.

'You wanted to see me, sir?'

'I did. I do,' he corrected himself. 'I want the inside information on Navrátil's dislike of Rada.'

Peiperová was surprised. Navrátil had disliked Rada for longer than she had been in Prague, but had Slonský only now noticed this?

'So far as I know, sir, it goes back to their days at the police academy.'

'But they weren't in the same cohort.'

'No, sir, but they knew each other slightly. Rada passed out with top marks in his year, but Jan has always maintained that he cheated on one of his assessments.'

'Did he indeed?'

This was what Slonský wanted to hear. Malfeasance of this kind might not be a sacking offence but it would be a very handy thing to keep up his sleeve if it could be substantiated.

'And Navrátil, of course, only came second in his year.'

'Yes, sir. That rankles a bit. He doesn't dispute that someone may have been better than him, just that if he had been a year older he would certainly have been in first place.'

'And does Rada mention this often?'

'No, sir. But if you look over his desk in Lieutenant's Doležal's office you'll see Rada's certificate hanging on the wall.'

Slonský could not remember when he had last visited Doležal's office. If he wanted to speak to his colleague he normally badgered him in a corridor or on the stairs where he was easier to intimidate.

'And has Navrátil ever intimated the exact nature of this skulduggery?'

'Not to me, sir.'

Navrátil had a very highly developed sense of right and wrong, which is quite handy in a policeman, thought Slonský, though it would have made him stick out like a sore thumb in the Vice Squad. Cheating in an examination was exactly the kind of thing that would have riled him, especially if it had gone undetected and unpunished. But how could Navrátil have any proof of this when he cannot have been in the room while the assessment was taking place? There was, of course, only one way to find out.

'Thank you for your help. Needless to say, not a word of this to Navrátil.'

Peiperová bit her lip. 'Sir, is he in trouble?'

'Trouble? Navrátil? Of course not. The lad leads a blameless life. He's the nearest thing to a living saint I've ever met. He is kind to old ladies, never forgets a birthday and even lets you beat him at tennis.'

Peiperová smiled. 'I think I would beat him however hard he tried, sir. And I remind him about birthdays.'

'Well, at least he's kind to old ladies without prompting.'

'Yes, sir.'

Slonský decided to come clean. 'Rada is at a loose end now that Lieutenant Doležal has decamped to Pardubice, and he has noticed that there will be a vacancy in my team when you desert us to work for the Director of Criminal Police.'

'Oh.'

'You may well say "Oh!" in that tone of voice, miss. I'm going to have to endure twelve months of Navrátil looking out of the window and whimpering as he pines for you with those big sad puppy eyes of his. If he starts moulting don't blame me.'

'So Rada is after my job?'

'He is.'

'And when my secondment is over?'

'You'll come back, if you know what's good for you, whatever little trinkets are offered by those in high places.'

'But Rada will expect to keep the job, sir.'

'Yes, he will. And we don't want to let him, do we? So it would be good for both of us if he never got the job in the first place; and since the key to that is whatever little snippet Navrátil is keeping to himself, it is in both our interests if you can winkle that out of him and tell me. I could always lock him in cell five and play my Frank Sinatra CDs until he cracks, but I suspect you will have ways of getting it from him that are more effective and less brutal. Do we have an agreement?'

'Yes, sir, we do. Leave it to me.'

# Chapter 7

The report from Dr Novák about the grenade was relatively unenlightening, in the sense that it confirmed what was already suspected. The grenade was standard Warsaw Pact issue dating from around 1966 with no distinguishing features.

Slonský slid it across the table to Dr Kohoutek who read it with interest.

'Amateurs,' he said at last.

'How do you mean, amateurs?'

'If your expert is right and this was an RGO series fragmentation grenade, perhaps an RGO-78, it would have two possible detonation methods. It can be set to explode on impact, or it can explode on a three to four second fuse. Unless you're a very good thrower, getting it to land in the centre of a two metre circle made by the mens' legs would be quite a feat. You'd have to be quite close to make sure of doing the job. Let's say you'd need to be within five metres. Then you've got four seconds to get out of the range of the explosion. This thing is lethal at twenty to thirty metres, so you've got to move. But fragments are often recovered up to a hundred metres away. It was completely impractical for the way it was used. Running in mud, in ordinary clothes, you'd be lucky to cover six metres a second. When the grenade went off, the thrower would only have made eighteen to twenty-four metres. However you look at it, he'd still be within fragmentation range.' Kohoutek took a slurp from his beer. 'I'd say there's a very good chance that whoever threw this was injured in the blast.'

Novák listened with interest as Slonský filled him in.

'Well, it's plausible. I'd defer to Dr Kohoutek given his reputation, but there's a difficulty with that supposition. If the man was injured, I'd have expected to find a definite pool of blood on the ground, and I didn't.'

'Couldn't it have been just part of the general carnage?'

'If it killed him, perhaps it wouldn't have been easy to read the signs, but it didn't. A significant injury means blood, and we bleed where we are. I suppose it's just possible that he was hit in the back and managed to keep his feet until he got outside the field. I didn't see anything that looked like someone going full length in the mud.'

'What about the noise?'

'Inner or middle ear disruption occurs in a quarter to a third of people near an explosion who aren't wearing ear protection.'

'Which means?'

'If his ears weren't pointing at the blast, it's more likely than not he's okay, but otherwise he may have some ringing in his ears.'

'Enough to need medical attention?'

'The fragments would be a bigger problem, Slonský. If he's close enough to injure his hearing, he's close enough to be turned into a steel porcupine. But there is one other possibility that has just occurred to me.'

'Which is?'

'I wonder if it's possible that the grenade was wedged between them and the pin was pulled out with a wire or string? That would allow the killer to put some distance between them and him.'

'Did we find the pin?'

'No, but then we didn't find about a third of the metal that must have been in the grenade. Maybe we need to go back with a metal detector and look again.'

'Well, if you do, be careful. It was a metal detector that started this whole thing off.'

Slonský was struggling. The Human Resources team were putting him through an intensive orientation session which involved a string of lectures and workshops. Slonský belonged to a generation that thought a "workshop" had to involve a lathe, and he was not at all clear what the difference was between a lecture and a workshop, since both appeared to involve earnest women shouting at him.

Although Slonský was refreshingly free of prejudices, treating everyone with the same degree of contempt whatever their race, creed or sexuality, he was finding it hard to express himself in acceptable language. He had spent nearly five minutes during the first written exercise trying to remember what the B in LGBT stood for and his attempt to sort a string of names for Roma into acceptable and unacceptable contained so many crossings out and arrows that it was well-nigh illegible.

The instructor announced that after a short coffee break they were going to go into a roleplay masterclass, leaving Slonský hoping that there would be a nice juicy murder somewhere in the next hour that would demand his immediate attention. If not, he was prepared to commit one, and he knew exactly who the likeliest victim was, just as soon as she got back from her short coffee break.

How was he going to resolve this disagreement between Kohoutek and Novák? Was he looking for someone with a back full of metal shards or not? Maybe it was worth checking out the hospitals and doctors near Holice in case anyone had shown up looking for first aid.

'Very well done indeed, Lieutenant Slonský!' he heard.

Glancing up, he suddenly realised that he had not been paying attention to the young policewoman sitting opposite him, but that did not seem to matter to the harridan with the mad hair who was conducting the training.

'You didn't interrupt and you allowed this poor woman to tell her story in her own time, whilst simultaneously showing your empathy by your facial expression. Plainly you were thinking hard about what she was telling you. Did everybody see that?'

There was a little ripple of applause.

'It's just experience,' Slonský declared modestly. 'You learn not to force things in some circumstances.'

It's lucky there is nobody here who knows me, he thought.


Once released from the training room Slonský hurried back to his desk. As he passed Captain Lukas' door he heard a summons.

'Do you have a moment?' Lukas asked.

'Of course, sir,' Slonský replied, hoping he would not forget the various things he had planned to set in train.

'I understand you've completed part one of your equality and diversity training.'

Slonský brandished his certificate.

'Excellent. And I'm pleased to say your medical report produced a higher classification than I was expecting. But then I can see you're losing weight.'

'You can?'

Slonský had not dared to step on a weighing machine in case the consequent disappointment were crushing, so it was good to hear that the change was visible.

'Keep up the good work. I just wanted to have a chat about the transition and your future plans for the department.'

Send Doležal to the back of beyond, blackmail Rada into resigning and get Dvorník neutered about summed it up, but Slonský thought it might be impolitic to say so just yet. 'Of course, sir. What did you want to discuss?'

'As I see it, we have some key dates. On 1st June Peiperová begins her twelve-month secondment to the Director of Criminal Police. Between ourselves, the Director is likely to be promoted to head up the whole force in September, so I imagine there will be a question about whether she will go with him.'

'Peiperová says he plans to take her, sir. He has already shared his expectations with her.'

'I see. Then I retire on 30th June. But to ease the handover it would be better if you took control while I was still here, so now that there is no further impediment to your promotion I propose that we should formally handover as soon as your captaincy documents are received, which should be in the next few days. Then I'll use my outstanding leave up.'

'I'd like to finish the Holice case first if I can, sir.'

'Of course. And the two may not be incompatible. But even if you haven't wrapped up the Holice enquiry I think it would be good to see you in full control by the start of June at the latest. Then you'll discover what kind of rubbish I've had to put up with over the years!'

Slonský was only too aware that he had been directly responsible for a good chunk of that rubbish with his obstinate refusal to hand in expenses claims that added up correctly. Before the advent of Navrátil anything that he typed had been a collage of fonts, inconsistent bullet lists and doubtful grammar.

'I'm already discovering some of that, sir. Doležal has been lobbying me to be made senior lieutenant and Rada wants to slip into Peiperová's place.'

'There's a certain tidiness in that, but I detect from your tone of voice that you have reservations.'

'Navrátil and Rada go together like vampires and garlic, sir. It seems that Navrátil believes that Rada may have cheated in his final examinations.'

Lukas frowned deeply. 'That is a very serious allegation. Does Navrátil have proof?'

'I'm still trying to ascertain that, sir.'

'Either way, if he believes it to be true — and he is a very honest and upright young man — it won't make for harmonious working.' Lukas tapped his pen on his notepad a few times while he thought. 'I assume you would like to keep Navrátil and persuade Rada that his future lies elsewhere?'

'Ideally. But I can't sack him on the basis of an as yet unsubstantiated allegation.'

'Heaven forbid. Certainly not. Quite improper.'

'And I haven't thought of anything else to do.'

Lukas leaned forward and lowered his voice. 'Then you mustn't do anything to Rada. You must let him make the first move.'

Slonský felt a compulsion to lean forward too. 'How?'

'By creating circumstances in which Rada will not want to stay. How do you think Rada would feel if Navrátil were promoted to lieutenant?'

Slonský felt as if a lightning bolt had passed through his brain. Of course! 'But Navrátil has only been here fifteen months. Normally he'd have to do at least two years, if not three.'

'Navrátil is one of our first degree entry officers. It is a new programme, Josef. Some elements of that were, perhaps, not entirely thought through.'

'I'm not sure I follow…'

'The rules that require a two or three year wait were designed for officers who may well have left school without a diploma of any kind. It would be ridiculous to apply them to someone like Navrátil who has completed a law degree. The graduate entry programme was devised because we were one of the few countries which did not apply an educational test to would-be policemen, so some needed a lot of training on the job. Navrátil doesn't, and that should be reflected in the time it takes him to get promotion.'

'You've convinced me, sir, but can you convince the powers that be?'

'I think the Director of Criminal Police will see the benefits of such a change when he is reminded that the happiness of his new Personal Assistant may depend upon it.'

Slonský's heart jumped, then sank. 'She'll be happy for Navrátil, but jealous for herself.'

'It wouldn't surprise me if the Director nominated her for promotion at the end of her year. It's happened before — just not for the likes of Kuchař. And even if he doesn't, you can when she returns. It gives her an added reason to want to come back.'

*I have misjudged you*, thought Slonský. *All these years I never realised you were as devious and scheming as the rest of us.* 'But that would give me four lieutenants, sir — Dvorník, Doležal, Navrátil and Peiperová — and I only have room for three.'

'True, but you'll have a year to find something for Doležal. Maybe he'll enjoy Pardubice and want to stay. Failing which…' Lukas opened the drawer of his desk and handed Slonský a leaflet. 'Food for thought?' he said.

'Oh, yes,' replied Slonský. 'Yes, indeed.'

# Chapter 8

Poznar's message was short and admirably to the point.

*Same place. 14:15.*

Slonský slipped out of the office without telling anyone where he was going, though he did mention to Sergeant Mucha that there was no point in phoning him for the next couple of hours because he would not pick up.

He opened the café door to find Poznar sitting with a coffee and a bowl of soup.

'That looks good,' Slonský remarked.

'I haven't had time for lunch. But actually it's as good as it looks. Let me get you one.' Poznar beckoned the waiter and gave the order. It was not until the waiter had returned to the counter that he continued. 'I've been talking to our experts on militant nationalist groups.'

'We have some then?'

'Militant nationalist groups? Plenty.'

'I meant experts on them.'

'A few. But the ones who know a lot do nothing and the ones who do a lot know nothing.'

'I thought that was true of all branches of government?'

Poznar smiled. 'Let's keep to the point, shall we? First, they say that there is a group in Pardubice claiming to be connected to the National Resistance movement.'

That was no surprise to Slonský. Everywhere you went there were young thugs who found neo-nazism attractive, usually because they liked uniforms and baiting Jews and Roma.

'This group,' Poznar continued, 'is almost entirely ineffectual. We've infiltrated them and it's no more than a talking shop.

But we're told that they made contact late last year with people from a kindred Slovak group who paid them a visit. The Slovaks were getting respectable results in local elections and our boys wanted to know how they had done it. Now, so far as we can discover, nothing much came of the meeting. The Slovaks didn't believe that Czechs had anything to teach them in return and the Czechs found the Slovaks arrogant and intolerant.'

'Neo-nazi Slovaks intolerant? I find that hard to believe,' Slonský interjected.

'But — and pay attention to this — the Slovaks apparently reported to their own supporters that they had been approached outside the meeting by a small clutch of Czechs who said that they were tired of democratic means and wanted to make a mark so that Czechs would realise there were true patriots among them.'

'We're all patriots, aren't we? I, for one, only drink Czech beer.'

'Don't we all? But this party intrigued the Slovaks because they weren't all the usual young lads. There were educated men and fellows in their forties, they thought.'

'And how do we know this?'

'Friends in Slovakia with big ears.'

Slonský nodded. The waiter had arrived with the soup and coffee so Slonský switched the conversation to Poznar's summer holiday plans for a moment until they were left alone again. 'Anyway — you were saying.'

'Now, we don't know who these Czechs were. Our infiltrator says that nobody he spoke to had heard about any such contact nor could they think who they might be. And we won't find out because our man got a bit careless and pushed too hard, with the result that he had to get out of town fast and was holed up in Germany for a while enjoying a bit of rest and recuperation. By an eerie coincidence your man Sedlák was looking for him on a charge of malicious wounding.'

Slonský's eyebrows attempted some gymnastics across his brow. 'Really? Who did he go for?'

'A nice fellow called Martin Svoboda. Svoboda wouldn't have said anything, only he turned up in hospital with a badly broken arm and a nasty gash in his forearm. He was also stunned, probably as a result of a thump to the head with something heavy, so he couldn't say much, but he was taken there by a man named Barták who claimed that Svoboda had been set upon by our man when the two of them were minding their own business while out for a stroll. The difficulty with this account was that a woman claimed that she had seen them trying the back doors of houses along a street behind hers and that our man appeared to have been hiding in an outhouse behind one of them. Barták had gone down a side passage when our chap broke cover and ran for the road, closely pursued by Svoboda. But, I'm delighted to say, as Svoboda turned the corner he seems to have inadvertently struck his head several times on a piece of steel shelving strut. He must have raised his arm to protect himself, hence the broken forearm and the gash that made him pull his arm out of the way. Barták made a statement at the hospital to Lieutenant Sedlák. Sedlák discovered that Svoboda was a person of interest to us and copied the report to our office, and someone decided that we needed to pull our man out.'

'Did you tell Sedlák this?'

'We wouldn't normally,' Poznar replied. 'Things get out, you see. Much easier if we just offer him every assistance short of actual help and thus ensure that our man is never caught.

Eventually the fuss dies down and Sedlák would have given up.'

'And did he?'

'The file was still open when he died, but these events were three or four months ago, and he had done nothing practical for much of that time.'

'That sounds like Sedlák. So do we know anything at all about these men?'

'Not really. We could do with implanting a man there to see if he can pick anything up, but in view of recent experience there's no appetite amongst my lot for doing so just yet. I don't have any proof that these people who badgered the Slovaks are connected in any way to your explosion, but I don't believe in coincidence, and here we have a group of unknown men expressing an interest in direct action, and you have someone who has access to a big bit of armour plated steel with a gun on the front. Suppose these men had found or stolen the gun? It was on the move because it had been stolen from the people who originally had it but weren't using it.'

Slonský dipped some bread in his soup and chewed reflectively. 'It's plausible, isn't it? They'd have to have found a gun that nobody had reported missing and that people had been very tight-lipped about for nearly forty years, but maybe somebody blabbed.'

'If you keep a secret for that long, why suddenly start talking about it?'

'Let's work forwards from 1968. You've got five or six people who know where that gun went. They have every reason to keep it to themselves, and secrecy becomes a habit. Until, say, the fall of Communism in 1989 you might still need the gun, so you say nothing. Presumably those men who were army age in 1968 would still be alive in 1989, so they could talk about it then, but it sounds as if they didn't. Here we are nearly twenty years later, and those men will be my age or older. Some may be dead. If they want to hand on the torch they have to find new people to tell. And the new people haven't lived under a government where saying the wrong thing can get you up against a wall wearing a blindfold. My generation was much better at keeping secrets because we had to be. Maybe it's got out now because new people have taken over the care of the thing?'

'Why wouldn't they just give the gun back to the Czech Army in 1989?' Poznar asked.

'I don't know. And until I do, it's a big hole in my theory.'

'I don't have a great deal of confidence in mine either. If it has been stolen you'd expect those who originally had it to be making efforts to get it back but we're not hearing of that. Of course, we're hampered by not having anyone on the ground there.'

An idea was forming in Slonský's head.


'Are you serious, sir?' Navrátil asked.

'Deadly serious.' Slonský reconsidered for a moment, then added, 'Maybe "Deadly" wasn't the best word to use there.'

'You want me to infiltrate a far right gang that has already tried to kill a police officer?'

'Well, that's not going to be a problem if you don't let on that you're a police officer.'

'Don't worry, I won't.'

'And I don't want you to become a member or anything like that. Just give the impression that you're sympathetic to their aims and see if they tell you anything.'

'But I'm not sympathetic to their aims.'

'Navrátil, when you were a little kid just starting school, did your teacher ever play that game where you all pretend to be trees?'

'Yes, of course.'

'There you are, then. You're a lot more like a right-wing terrorist than you are a tree, so if you pulled that off pretending to be a neo-nazi should be a piece of cake.'

'And how do I convince them I'm one of them? You can't just sit in a bar asking strangers "I'm new in town. Do you know where the neo-nazis hang out?", can you?'

'Obviously you have to be more subtle than that. Poznar will give you some tips. He's coming up with a cover story for you.'

'Sir, be straight with me. Isn't this a bit dangerous?'

Slonský sighed. 'Of course it is, lad. It's more dangerous than a Prague taxi-driver in a hurry. But I wouldn't ask if it wasn't necessary. We'll tell Doležal what you're up to so that he doesn't get in your way or throw a fit if he sees you. And he'll provide backup if you need it urgently, though until the very last you communicate through this office. It won't be healthy to be seen talking to the police.'

'I'm not sure I like that phrase "until the very last", sir.'

'Don't be difficult, Navrátil. Are you going to help or not?'

'And if I say no…?'

'Clearly I'll have to order you to do it. But I'd rather not.'

'Is that so you'll feel less guilty if anything happens to me?'

'Nothing will make me feel less guilty, Navrátil. And even if I tried to escape any guilt, I'm sure Peiperová will keep reminding me. And, if I'm honest, I'm more scared of her disapproval than yours.'

Navrátil looked pensive. 'I'll do it, sir, on one condition.'

'Which is?'

'You explain it all to Kristýna.'

'What's your name?' barked Poznar.

'Michal Ondráček.'

'Occupation?'

'Postgraduate doctoral student, Charles University.'

'Supervisor?'

'Professor Jakub Hofmann.'

'Very good, Navrátil. On to the next part.'

Navrátil relaxed. Learning somebody else's name was the easy part; not responding to his own was the tricky bit. That, and the prospect of not being able to communicate with Peiperová for an unknown period of time.

Poznar dropped a battered manila folder on the desk.

'This is a nicely dog-eared first draft of your Ph.D. thesis. It would be as well to read it, given that our technical people have gone to great lengths to create it. The essence of this is that Professor Hofmann didn't like it. Your thesis title is "Czech cultural identity since 1945" and you'll see from his scribbles that he liked the bit up to 1989, he was reasonably happy with the chapter up to the separation from Slovakia in 1993, and he thought only a few alterations were needed in the chapters from 1993 to our accession to the European Union in 2004, but he was deeply unhappy with the chapters after that, because he said you had underplayed the desire to be European, as evidenced by the 77% vote in favour at the EU referendum. So he wants you to do some field work asking people who voted in favour whether they think they are primarily European or Czech. You have to do it, and he has suggested the Pardubice and Holice area as a good testing ground, but you'll tell anyone who listens that the point of your research was to reinforce the importance of being Czech and not losing that uniqueness within the European Union. With luck, that will give anyone who hears you the chance to agree and perhaps somebody will introduce you to a militant such as would join Our Home. Any questions?'

Navrátil looked unhappily at a couple of pages and noted the copious comments in red ink. Even though it was not actually his thesis he felt Ondráček's pain.

'Is Ondráček real, sir?'

'No, we can't use a real student's identity in case someone knows him. But if anyone enquires they'll find Michal Ondráček in the university files. Fortunately the university computers weren't too difficult for our guys to get into. Professor Hofmann isn't real either, but he has a webpage if anyone goes on to the university website and puts his name in the search box. You might want to take a look in case you ever need to describe him. Scruffy, curly hair, red complexion, round gunmetal-coloured glasses he wears partway down his nose, straggly beard.'

'Suppose somebody wants to speak to him, sir?'

'Here's his business card. That telephone number at the bottom diverts to us, and we'll know it's someone wanting Hofmann. Whoever answers will know what to do. If you need to call us, this is the simple way to do it. Just tell us you're Ondráček and we'll know to whom we're really speaking.'

'I've spoken to Lieutenant Doležal this afternoon and explained that you'll be working there undercover, but I haven't told him what exactly you're doing,' Slonský chipped in.

'Doležal will keep out of your way. If you need him, contact him through us,' warned Poznar. 'Doing it any other way could put you both in danger. Remember that these people have already killed to keep their secret.'

'Believe me, I won't forget,' Navrátil assured them.

'We won't leave you there indefinitely but we'll have to rely on your reports to decide whether trying to infiltrate them is a dead duck. Expect to be there for a month at least. We've got you a room in a private house such as a graduate student might be able to afford and we've paid for two weeks up front.'

'After that?' Navrátil asked, hoping that he was not going to be expected to pay for everything and reclaim it when he got back to Prague.

'We've got you a bank debit card in your new name. We'll monitor the account and keep it topped up. You'll always have five thousand crowns in there. If you need more there's also a credit card here. Don't go wild with it. I know you've got to eat but I don't want to find you've been on extended pub crawls or buying the company of loose women.'

'Anyone less likely than Navrátil to do either of those would be hard to imagine,' Slonský interjected. 'He's more disposed towards blowing the lot on votive candles and presents for his girlfriend.'

'Girlfriend?' said Poznar. 'How are you going to explain where you are to her?'

'She's another police officer,' Slonský said. 'Soon to be personal assistant to the Director of Criminal Police. She can be trusted.'

Poznar relaxed. 'Well, that's good. I'd hate to have her banging on my door every few minutes. You won't be able to contact her directly. Even letters may be intercepted.'

'She lives in the police barracks,' said Navrátil, 'so I didn't expect to be able to write. Maybe I can phone her.'

'Just remember you may be overheard. Tell her nothing about the job,' said Poznar.

'I won't and she wouldn't expect it, sir.'

'I'd be sparing. Once or twice a week, ideally when she isn't on duty.'

'Very good, sir.'

'And remember that if they're well connected, and we don't know that they aren't, they may be listening in on your phone, so you might put her in danger if they realise that she's a police officer too.'

'I won't do that,' Navrátil claimed.

There was an awkward pause.

'Any questions?' asked Poznar.

'I don't think so,' Slonský replied.

'I was asking Navrátil.'

'Oh — well, have you, lad?'

'No, sir. I'll get going in the morning.'

'Very good. Stick to public transport. We don't want anyone booby-trapping your car.'

Navrátil liked this assignment less and less.


Peiperová felt much the same way when Navrátil broke the news.

'It could be dangerous,' she said.

'I know,' Navrátil responded.

'Promise me you won't get hurt?'

'That's a bit difficult to promise, isn't it? I'll be very, very careful.'

'I'm not going to enjoy not being able to talk to you whenever I want.'

'Me neither.'

'Just promise me if there's any trouble you won't be brave?'

'You want me to be a coward?'

'Yes, because cowards keep safer than brave people. If rough stuff starts I want you to run away as fast as you can.'

'Don't worry,' said Navrátil. 'That's exactly what I was planning to do.'

'What's eating you?' Valentin asked Slonský.

'Hm? Oh, Navrátil's got a job to do and it could be dangerous.'

'Then shouldn't you be doing it?'

'I'm needed here. And he's much more nondescript than me. I don't want to be antisocial but I can't talk about it.'

'You're talking about it now.'

'Only in general terms. If it got out I was speaking to a journalist there'd be hell to pay.'

'You're not. You're talking to me as your oldest friend.'

'Who is a journalist.'

'Well, technically, perhaps. But you're speaking to me in my private rather than my professional capacity. Or, more accurately, not speaking to me.'

'Things are just a bit tense at the moment, old pal. I'd feel happy if I knew a bit more about what we're letting Navrátil in for.'

'He's a bright lad. He can afford to rely on his wits.'

'Oh, he's intelligent enough. One of the brightest policemen I've ever met, though I'm not sure that's much of a commendation. But he's too trusting and innocent. He's just not suspicious enough. Now, Peiperová is another matter. She can spot a lie from a hundred metres.'

'Send her, then.'

'You can't send a woman into that kind of danger! All sorts of things that don't bear thinking about could happen.'

Valentin took a slug of his iced water, having removed the slice of lime from the rim of the glass to make it look more manly. 'You know best. But young women today bang on about equality, so I'd have thought that has to include an equal right to the nasty jobs too.'

'You may have a point. But even if she begged me to be allowed to go, she's due in the Office of the Director of Criminal Police for 366 days as from 1st June, and he'd have my anus for a novelty inkwell if I let anything happen to her before then.'

'She hasn't got out of it, then?'

'I don't see how she can. In theory she has a choice, but in practice...'

'Ah, yes. The good old-fashioned Czech way.'

'We had a choice under communism, didn't we? Do what they want or spend a few years in a labour camp thinking about what you might have done differently.'

'I never actually went to prison. There was a time when having been jailed was quite a badge of honour in the Journalists' Union.'

'Yes, but not until the ones who did the jailing had gone.'

Valentin took another glug. 'Can't you wire Navrátil up with cameras and microphones and things?' he suggested. 'There was a documentary on television the other night when they sent an undercover reporter to look at practices in a vegetable canning factory, and he was a walking film studio.'

'When do you see television? You're in here every night.'

'I recorded it on my video recorder. And I'm not here every night. I missed 5th April.'

'Did you?'

'Tummy trouble. Flooding out of me like...'

'Yes, I get the point. Anyway, we daren't kit Navrátil up with all that. If he gets detected he'd be in real trouble.'

'Well, he'd be in real trouble anyway, by your account. What more can fitting him up with some technology cause?'

# Chapter 9

If Navrátil had been taken aback by the early morning phone call from his boss ordering him to come to the office before leaving, he was more amazed to be directed to the technical services department, and was now standing in his underwear as Slonský and Technician First Class Spehar discussed his complaint that while he understood the reason for fitting him with a video camera and microphone, keeping the battery pack down his boxer shorts was surprisingly uncomfortable, not to mention that it was getting quite warm.

'Can't he just put the battery in his jacket pocket?' asked Spehar.

'You can see the bulge.'

'We could give him a kit with an integral rechargeable battery.'

'How long does it run between charges?'

'Four to six hours, maybe.'

'Can he turn it off to save the battery?'

'Yes, but it draws attention to you. And the camera is concealed in a lapel badge which might lead people to wonder why he's always wearing it.'

Slonský scratched his head. 'You're the one who has to wear it, lad. What do you think?'

'Can I put my trousers back on while we talk, sir?'

'Go on, then. We've admired the sharp creases in your boxer shorts long enough.'

Spehar left the room for a moment. The two detectives could hear the unmistakable sound of a shelf tumbling from a cupboard as items were moved around. Spehar reappeared with a battered light brown briefcase in his hand.

'I'll sort that out later,' he muttered, glancing over his shoulder at a passageway littered with objects as diverse as a large parasol, a goaltender's hockey stick and a supermarket trolley. 'This may be the answer to our problem.'

'An antique briefcase?' Slonský commented.

'Yes, but not just any antique briefcase. This one has cameras built into the handle.'

'Which way does the camera point?' asked Navrátil.

'Both ways. You decide which one is switched on by squeezing the handle at the corresponding end. That's the beauty of this model. You don't have to carry it in any particular way just so long as you squeeze the handle when you want to record. There's also a microphone. You switch that on by pressing the lock in while the briefcase flap is open. But if the camera is on the microphone automatically comes on as well. Really clever piece of work.'

'Battery life?' asked Slonský, testing the weight of it in expectation that it would be absurdly heavy.

'All day. Say, sixteen hours.'

Spehar reached inside the case and produced a flat black slab about thirty centimetres by ten. 'This is the battery.'

'It's disconnected,' Slonský pointed out.

'This is the spare. It has two. The other is under the floor of the case secured by press studs which double as the terminals. You leave one on charge while the other is in use.'

'It looks battered enough to belong to a graduate student, I'll give you that,' Slonský conceded. 'What do you think, Navrátil?'

'Anything that doesn't involve batteries in my underwear sounds a better bet to me, sir.'

'Fine. We'll have it, Spehar. Don't bother to wrap it, we'll take it as it is.'

Navrátil loaded his new briefcase with his thesis, some pads, pens and pencils and his personal pencil sharpener. Peiperová looked on anxiously as he checked the contents of his suitcase one last time, a redundant act given that he had made a checklist and checked it twice more since it was packed, but one that helped him to control his emotions by giving him something to do.

'I've got to go and see Mucha about something,' said Slonský. 'I'll see you downstairs in ten minutes.'

'Anything I can help with, sir?' Peiperová enquired.

Slonský stopped in his tracks. 'No, because there isn't actually anything I want to see Mucha about. It was just a tactful way of allowing you to say your goodbyes with a modicum of privacy.'

Peiperová blushed. She could hardly be blamed for failing to suspect that Slonský was being tactful, since the last known comparable instance had occurred before she reached high school.

'We appreciate the thought, sir,' Navrátil answered, and Slonský nodded curtly and shut the door behind himself.

'Well, I suppose this is it,' said Navrátil.

'I suppose so,' said Peiperová. She had some difficulty in making the remark, because her bottom lip seemed to have a mind of its own. Despite her fierce efforts, tears erupted from her eyes and ran down her finely sculpted cheekbones. Navrátil wrapped her in his arms and held her very tightly so that she would not see his own eyes glistening. She stroked the back of his head and kissed the side of his neck, after which his lips found hers and no further conversation ensued for the remainder of the ten minutes.

When Navrátil got to Holice, the woman at the reception desk gave him a photocopied plan of the town centre and marked his temporary home on it, cleverly placing the cross in the middle of the road and thus giving no indication whether to look to the left or the right. Navrátil found it and discovered that his room was unexpectedly airy, the result of an extension having been built at the back. He had windows on each side and the kitchen was directly beneath him, ensuring that he was never deprived of the smell of cabbage. Since the window to the left was only a few metres from the house next door, that one had frosted glass, but otherwise he had pleasant views to enjoy so long as he kept his eyes on the horizon and ignored the intervening streets.

One of Navrátil's best qualities was his willingness to do the job whatever his personal feelings about the task he had been given. Never mind that he was miserable about the separation from Peiperová and the surroundings in which he was placed; disregarding his misgivings about the possible, if unquantifiable, risk of the task in hand, Navrátil gave a deep sigh, took his briefcase in hand and set out into town to see what he could see.

Slonský sucked in his stomach to the greatest degree possible.

'That's all very well,' said the tailor, 'but sometime during the next three years you're going to need to breathe out.'

'Sorry. Just allowing for the weight I'm going to lose.'

'Yes, they all say that,' murmured the tailor.

Slonský glanced in the mirror and was not enamoured of the spectacle that faced him. He had spent much of his career trying to get into a job where he no longer needed to wear uniform, and now, after so many years in which his uniform only came out of the closet for state occasions and disciplinary hearings he was about to go back into it. Part of his negotiation with the Director of Criminal Police was that he could wear his own clothes when investigating crime, because he had been able to retain some casework. Unlike Lukas, who had found himself behind a desk all the time, Slonský had planned to farm out some of the administrative work to people who did it better than he would to leave himself time to continue detecting. During Lukas' sick leave this had meant Peiperová taking on most of the administration in her newly invented position of Acting Acting Captain, and by common consent the department had never run so efficiently. However, the Director of Criminal Police giveth and the Director of Criminal Police taketh away, and having agreed to Slonský's cunning wheeze he had then removed Peiperová for a year, thus ensuring that Slonský would spend far more time behind a desk than he was expecting. Since he was also expected to wear uniform for some inter-departmental meetings, he had dug it out of the dark recesses of his wardrobe to discover that it had apparently belonged to a much smaller man and had changed colour due to a fine layer of dust that stubbornly refused to move. He had invested a small fortune in having it professionally cleaned only to find that it seemed not to match anyone else's when it came back.

Mucha had hung it on one of the hooks next to his own. 'Have you tried ringing the police museum to see if they'd like it?' he had asked.

Since a change of rank was involved Slonský had been entitled to the services of the ladies who did the sewing for the police. He was unsure exactly where they were these days;

when he had been promoted to lieutenant it had been two grandmas in the basement who had sewn on his insignia for him, encouraged by a small bottle of plum brandy in the pocket which had done wonders in elevating him up the queue of work but did nothing for the accuracy of the alignment of the stars on his epaulettes. Lukas had come to his rescue by authorising a completely new uniform for him, and the tailor was now checking whether any of the stock uniforms would fit well enough. It soon became clear that the peculiarities of Slonský's physique would require some alterations.

'It'll be a week,' said the tailor. 'Promise me you won't lose significant amounts of weight in the meantime.'

'I'll try not to,' Slonský replied, hoping that his tone conveyed his disappointment at having to make that commitment.

Navrátil had wandered around the centre of town for a while and selected a café that looked promising. There was a mixed clientele and it was busy much of the time, or at least busier than most other places he had seen, and it seemed to be run by the owner as opposed to a manager.

She listened attentively to his proposal and agreed enthusiastically. Navrátil could set up at a table and invite people to complete his questionnaire there, in exchange for which he would pay for a coffee for them. The number of completed questionnaires should tally with the number of till slips, and they would settle up at the end of each day.

He had explained that he had to collect a stratified sample, which was a phrase that he had picked up somewhere, and which he interpreted to mean he needed equal numbers of men and women, a set number in each age group and an indication of how they had voted in the EU membership referendum, though they could decline to answer that. As he had suspected, the owner hinted to her regulars that if they went over to speak to the nice young man in the corner for a few minutes he would pay for their coffee, and during what was left of the afternoon he collected a dozen questionnaires.

The next step was to have something to eat in a bar and make a similar arrangement, but he could not possibly pay for a beer for everyone given the deep affection that Czechs have for the golden liquid. However, he cut a deal under which a platter of bread, salami and cheese was prepared and he could hand that out until it ran out. He swiftly decided that assembling an open sandwich or two himself was preferable to letting the ravening hordes make their own.

He was surprised at how many people were prepared to answer his questionnaire. He had expected a cold shoulder but folks were very happy to tell him what they thought. Not only that, but several then fetched their friends to enjoy a free sandwich in exchange for telling a complete stranger what they thought, always a popular pastime in the Czech Republic even without the added incentive of a bite to eat.

By the end of the first evening Navrátil had twenty-one questionnaires. The following day he started earlier and as a result collected a further thirty, including one from Doležal who dropped into the café at lunchtime and betrayed no sign that he had ever seen Navrátil before. At the counter Doležal insisted on paying for his own coffee and showed his badge by way of explanation.

'We're not allowed to accept gifts,' he said. 'It might look bad later.' He gave a slim and insincere smile, pulled the door open and walked back to his car.

The owner came across to Navrátil's table and took out her cloth to polish the top. 'That man,' she said quietly. 'He's a cop. Be careful.'

'Thanks for the tip,' Navrátil answered.

'I haven't seen him before. I wonder why he's come to Holice?'

'Plain clothes,' Navrátil commented. 'Must be a detective.'

'I suppose. But what is he detecting?'

'Search me,' answered Navrátil, hoping that he wasn't going as red as he usually did when he was trying to tell a lie.

'I wonder if it's something to do with that explosion the other day?'

Navrátil decided to play dumb. 'Explosion? What explosion?'

'Some people with metal detectors got blown up by an old bomb in a field on the edge of town.'

'Really? You'd have thought that would have been on the news?'

'It was. Don't you watch television?'

'I don't have one. It would only distract me from my work. I've got to get my thesis finished by September and my professor wasn't happy with my first draft.'

'That's a shame.'

'Yes. A lot of work had gone into it, but I'm afraid he's a rabid European. He's quite happy to be European rather than Czech.'

'Can't you be both?'

'Yes. I think I am, for example. But he can't see anything wrong with the EU and nothing to be especially proud of in being Czech.'

'Well, if he comes in you point him out to me, dear, and I'll have some words with him. And they'll all be in good old-fashioned Czech.'

115

She returned to her counter leaving Navrátil to ponder why she thought he needed to be careful when the police were around.

Peiperová was unhappy. She would have been unhappy at being separated from Navrátil anyway, but her misery was enhanced by her doubts about whether she was doing the right thing by going to work for the Director of Criminal Police.

'You can't back out now, lass,' Slonský told her. 'Black mark on your record. Not that it matters a lot, because I've got several, but more to the point you'd get a seriously annoyed boss who'll always be above you. Unless you shoot him, I suppose, but that's not a great career move if you get caught.'

'No, I'll have to go through with it. But I wanted to check you're not mad at me, sir. I'd like to think that I'll be welcomed back after my year.'

'Indeed you will. Don't worry about that. I have big plans for this department, and you're definitely part of them.'

'Thank you, sir. Only Rada has been hinting that he expects to get my job…'

'Has he now? Well, you and I discussed that, didn't we? I'll have to have a little chat with Rada.' Slonský had just been about to add "Don't you worry your pretty little head" when he remembered that it was one of the things the Equality and Diversity training had told him was a no-no these days. 'In the meantime, young lady, concentrate on impressing your new — and extremely temporary — boss as much as you've impressed me.'

Peiperová smiled. It was a weak smile, but a genuine one. 'Thank you, sir. I feel happier now, sir.' She put a hand on the door handle but was checked by Slonský's barking of her name.

'One other thing. It would be good if you dropped by once in a while for a chat when you're off duty. I'll probably still be here because we work longer hours than the folks in the deep pile carpet corridor.'

'I will, sir.'

'Good. That way you may recognise me in a year's time when I'm reduced to a sack of bones.'

Slonský considered his next course of action for a full twenty seconds. His initial plan was to stomp along the corridor and give Rada a piece of his mind, but a little voice at the back of his brain told him that Rada was acting like this out of insecurity and that the young Slonský would probably have done the same thing. The insecurity was probably also behind the cheating, though the young Slonský would not have done that, not because he was outstandingly moral but because the young Slonský was not inclined to give a toss about most things.

Instead he picked up the phone and dialled the Pardubice station, where they told him Lieutenant Doležal was at Holice, so he dialled Holice, where they thought he might be at Pardubice. He called Doležal's mobile phone, only to find that it went unanswered. He left a message and within a minute he received a text message in reply.

*Will come out and call you in ten minutes. D.*

Curious, thought Slonský, but he took advantage of the intermission to fetch himself a coffee and look longingly at the pastries.

'You told me to refuse to sell you any of those,' Dumpy Anna said.

'I can look, can't I? Anyway, when did you last do what a man told you?'

'Good point. Do you want one?'

Slonský sighed in resignation. 'Get thee behind me, Satan. Just the coffee, love.'

'Are you sickening for something?'

'Just trying to lose some weight.'

'You said. I can see a difference in you already.'

'You can?' said Slonský brightly.

'Oh, yes. You're much more miserable now.'

Slonský's phone was ringing as he reached the top of the stairs, so he ran the last few metres, ensuring that he slopped hot coffee down his shirt. He still missed the call, but Peiperová had recently shown him how to return the last call so he put his new skill to work and was rewarded with Doležal's voice.

'Where were you when I called?' asked Slonský.

'At the station.'

'They said you weren't.'

'I spend a lot of time hiding in the toilet.'

'That bad, is it?'

'You can't imagine. The captain is an ogre.'

'Worse than me?'

'Ten times.'

'Quite a compliment for me there.'

'There's no organisation, no initiative. More to the point, something stinks.'

'In the toilet?'

'No, in the department.'

'Really? Tell me more.'

'That deputy mayor, Veselý, is part of a consortium building a huge shopping mall. They've been given by the municipality in exchange for a stake. But so far as I can discover he's nowhere near being able to fund it himself, so I suspect he's a front man for someone else. I've briefed Klinger who is trying to find out who is bankrolling it.'

There were officers who would have bawled Doležal out for going to a senior officer behind their backs. Slonský was not one of them. To his way of thinking, this saved him some work and he could toddle upstairs whenever he wanted for a progress report straight from the horse's mouth, which was distinct from that part of a horse that he usually invoked to describe senior officers.

'Good. But they've got fraud people in Pardubice, haven't they?'

'I don't know who can be trusted yet. Veselý is buddies with Captain Forman at Holice and nobody seems at all interested about the plain fact that it will never make money. If you were going to build it why not do it in Pardubice, where you've got more people and it's nearer to Prague?'

'Lots of free land?'

'That's another thing. There are no eviction or rehousing orders relating to the people who live on the site. They know nothing. Veselý tried to pretend to me that nobody lived there but I've been to visit them.'

'If it's council land the council would have to rehouse them.'

'Yes, but Veselý says they're already clearing the site. These old folks are going to be given just a day or two to pack up.'

'I don't like the sound of it. Everyone deserves better treatment than that. Except people I arrest, of course.'

'Then there's the explosion. I'd have expected a lot of effort being that one of our own was killed. I know you're in charge but usually you'd see local officers sending in anything that might be useful. Instead they don't even seem to talk about it.'

'Maybe they think that's why you're there.'

'If so, you'd expect they'd talk to me, but they're not welcoming.'

'You think it's suspicious?'

'Not necessarily,' Doležal conceded. 'I think it may just be that there's a complete lack of effective leadership.'

'Perhaps you'll change things.'

'I don't think I can. I came here thinking I'd get some good experience for when I return. If it went really well, I might even want to stay here, I thought. But I hope we get this sorted soon or I'll go mad.'

This was definitely not what Slonský wanted to hear, unless Doležal meant the word "mad" literally, in which case he could be removed because the police did not allow mad people to stay in post — at least, not among the lower ranks. At colonel level and above, of course, you could be completely out of your tree and nobody would comment.

'What's your captain's name?' asked Slonský.

'Vondra.'

Slonský wrote it down. 'I'll have a word with the Director of Criminal Police. He owes me a favour seeing as he's taking Peiperová off me. Let's see if he can put a boot up Vondra's fundament.'

'I don't want any unpleasantness,' Doležal commented.

'I am Mr Diplomacy,' Slonský answered. 'However, this was not the main reason for ringing. Your lad Rada — he's finished his mentorship time with you, hasn't he?'

'He came in February 2005, so he's been with me twenty-seven months.'

'He wants to work with me to fill in for Peiperová, but if he's ready to move onwards and upwards I wouldn't want to hold him back. And strictly you should get a new trainee when you come back. How do you think he has done?'

Doležal needed to collect his thoughts. 'Frankly, based on his performance, I've no idea how he came out top of his class.'

'Ah, I can answer that. He cheated.'

'He cheated? How?' Doležal asked.

'I don't know. I'm waiting for details.'

'Then he should be disciplined. We don't want any untrustworthy police officers.'

'Quite right,' Slonský said. 'We've already got as many as we can handle. There are no vacancies.'


Dr Novák found Slonský and came straight to the point.

'Your man Kohoutek seems to have been vindicated.'

'Really?' said Slonský.

'We completed a finger search of the field.'

'How many fingers did you find?'

'Very droll. It's a search using fingers, not for fingers. We've mapped every metal fragment we found and it looks as if we have probably tracked 96% of the residual mass of the grenade.'

'What's that, then? The last Mass of the day when all the real priests have gone home?'

Novák expressed some exasperation with a deep sigh. Actually, he enjoyed comments like that which gave him the opportunity for some impromptu teaching.

'When a grenade explodes it obeys the laws of physics. Mass — or what an unscientific character like you calls, inaccurately, weight — cannot be created. Some of it remains unchanged, some is converted into energy, and some will be transformed into matter that will have dissipated by the time we come to collect it. Converted into gas, for example. If we know the composition of the grenade we can calculate how much could be retrievable after an explosion, and that's the residual mass.

Of course, there are unknowns, like the exact proportions of explosive material to casing in the particular grenade in question, so it's only an estimate.'

'If you can tell me what the unknowns are, how can they be unknowns?' Slonský demanded. Had Novák been able to see Slonský's face he would have seen the detective adopting his most guileless and innocent expression as if he genuinely wanted to know the answer to his question.

'They are unknown in their physical aspects, not their existence, Slonský, in the same way that if a rat enters your kitchen you'll know that a rat has been there but not whether it was large or small, black or brown. In fact, you'll know nothing about the rat at all.'

'I'll know one thing,' said Slonský.

'Oh, yes?'

'Yes. The rat will be disappointed because he'll have found damn all to eat there.'

'Let us put aside this persiflage, Slonský, while I tell you what you've been pestering me to find out for you. The debris extended for nearly sixty metres but the majority of it lay within a fifteen to twenty metre circle. This may have been influenced by the bodies absorbing a high proportion close to the locus of the explosion.'

'Locus of…?'

'The place where it went bang. A number of the metal fragments are bloodstained. We don't yet have full details of the analyses, but I can tell you one useful thing. There are at least five different people involved.'

'Four victims and one other?' Slonský asked.

'Yes. His identity is another of those unknowns we were talking about.'

'His?'

'It's a man. There are some tissue cells on a number of fragments we found in a cluster about twenty metres from the blast. Assuming that none of the known victims crawled away and came back again, I'm hypothesising that those cells belong to whoever threw the grenade. Anyway, I've sent them for DNA analysis despite the fact that I've had a memorandum from high places questioning why I'm likely to overspend my budget substantially.'

'I should blame criminals,' Slonský responded. 'That's what I do. They're exceeding their workplan.'

Novák snorted. 'That may have worked before 1989, Slonský, but it won't now.'

'I don't know. It seems to convince Captain Lukas.'

'Ha! Soon it'll be you who has to deal with subordinates trying it on.'

'Can you be both subordinate and insubordinate?' mused Slonský.

'I don't know,' said Novák, 'but if anyone is in a position to answer that it's you.'

# Chapter 10

The Director of Criminal Police was a perfect gentleman toward Peiperová. One or two of the other girls had hinted that everyone in the top corridor liked being surrounded by young women for unprofessional reasons, but so far he had not attempted to lay a finger on her. At her mother's insistence she always carried a sturdy hat-pin, though she doubted whether she possessed the mettle to stick it where her mother had suggested. Navrátil would have been exempt from such retribution, but he had not laid a hand on her either. Navrátil was very old school about what he called "that sort of thing". About three weeks after her year as Personal Assistant was due to end she and Navrátil were to become one, and Navrátil was determined that they would remain two right up until 21st June. Slonský had not helped matters when he had announced that while he respected Navrátil's views on sex before marriage, he was not at all sure that the young man was okay with sex *after* marriage either, and it would be as well for her to check where he stood on that. Despite the feeling that her strings were being pulled she had done so, and Navrátil had launched into a touching and emotional description of the anticipated joys of the marriage bed that left her feeling that she was under some pressure not to make it the greatest disappointment of his life. One of her girlfriends told her that her own boyfriend was a considerate tiger in bed; Peiperová feared that Navrátil would turn out to be an amenable kitten.

Peiperová was getting used to being left on her own. Trying to divide her time between orientation in her new role and tidying up her old one, she was struggling with both, but doggedly ploughing on. From time to time her thoughts turned to the explosion at Holice and she would find herself feeling deeply uneasy that there was something she should have noticed but had somehow overlooked; and she would think very hard about the evidence that she had collected before falling into a depressed and worried mood as she pondered how Navrátil was coping with the separation.

The separation was currently a matter of less concern to Navrátil than the state of his bladder. Coffee and beer were working it hard each day and he was beginning to wonder whether it was medically possible to wear your waterworks out. But, on the plus side, he was getting some very encouraging responses and it seemed likely that the contact that he had expected to take weeks might arrive in the very near future.

He had taken to having a late afternoon nap as a means of making it through to the end of the evening in the bar and decided that he could do with a run to shake off the lethargy of sitting all day nibbling on unhealthy food. Having carefully locked his room he pulled his sweatshirt over his head, stepped out into the street and began to run.

The run was not too hard so he completed it by sprinting the last four hundred metres, other pedestrians permitting, and as he let himself into his room he could see the trap he had left had been sprung. He had dragged the rug over to the door and carefully closed it with one corner of the rug lapped up the door. The idea was that if anyone went into the room they would push the rug back, realise that this would give the game away, and therefore flatten it out in what they would presume was its original position.

And that was exactly what he was looking at now. The ballpoint pen he had left pointing to the third line of his notes was now two lines further down the page. Reaching under the bed he checked his bag and could see that someone had opened it and rummaged inside, but they did not appear to have detected the false bottom.

Somebody seemed to be interested in him. He was glad that he had ensured that there was no evidence that he was a policeman and that his mobile phone was clipped to his waistband. It contained no real pointers to his work, unless you knew that "JS" was Slonský and "Kristýna" was Peiperová, but there were one or two texts in his correspondence with her that he would not have wanted anyone else to read due to their extremely affectionate character. Needless to say, Peiperová had written them.

Slonský opened the large navy blue folder and turned to page 135.

The instructor had been keen to impress upon the class the importance of promoting equality and diversity. Glancing around she had fastened her gaze on Slonský, who was clearly the oldest officer candidate in the room.

"Give me an example of diversity in the police,' she commanded.

Slonský responded at once. 'We employ officers ranging from the highly competent to the downright bloody useless,' he said.

Four hours of hell had followed, during which he had, among other things, had to play the role of a young woman officer negotiating reduced hours so she could look after her child, following which he took the opportunity of the "Personal Reflection Period" afterwards to express the view that her superior was a human latrine who should have immediately agreed to her reasonable request without all that pleading. Asked to complete a questionnaire about sources of information to which witnesses and complainants could be directed in a range of circumstances, he had bracketed them all together and written "Sergeant Mucha will know" at the bottom, defending himself under questioning with the additional information that Sergeant Mucha knows everything.

In preparation for the next session Slonský had been directed to read the regulations relating to holiday and sick leave, which was why he had the dark blue folder open at page 135. Without the support of pastries he slogged through to the end of page 139, at which point he decided it must be time to see if Valentin was in the bar as usual.

'Crime fighting going okay?' asked his friend.

'We don't actually do that any longer,' Slonský explained. 'The police exists in order to sympathise with the victims of crime, assure them that they have a shoulder to lean on and then make sure our subordinates get home in time for some quality hours with their loved ones during which they can forget work and the body they've just seen with its feet sawn off.'

'Stop me if I'm wrong, but you've been training again, haven't you?'

'How did you guess?'

'Did you learn anything today?' Valentin asked.

'I learned that my instructor uses enough lacquer to ensure that her hair will stay up longer than the Berlin Wall, that I am a "culturally insensitive dinosaur" and that officers can't bring their babies to work but are entitled to breast feed them in privacy if they do.'

'I find it hard to imagine that anyone told you that you were "culturally insensitive".'

'I know. I was shocked. It's just not true.'

'I wasn't questioning its truth, just that anyone dared to say it to you.'

'Well, they did. And I'm not insensitive at all. The dragon can't point to a single question I got wrong. She's just making presuppositions based on my age, sex and experience. I'm being stereotyped and I don't like it.'

'Never mind. Today is one of my alcohol days so I'll allow you to buy me a beer. Have one yourself too.'

'That's very good of you. I'll do that.' Slonský attracted a waiter's eye and placed their order.

'I haven't see Navrátil for a day or two,' Valentin observed.

'Working undercover. Don't ask.'

'In Holice?'

'I said don't ask.'

'That'll be to do with the explosion, then. Is he getting anywhere?'

Slonský breathed deeply to compose himself. 'I can't tell you. It's in the nature of undercover work that they don't keep ringing the police.' Slonský stared deep into his glass. 'You already know somebody is wandering free with a big motorised gun. Apparently it can heave a shell the size of my forearm over fifteen kilometres, and they've probably got thirty of them loaded up and the rest of the crate hidden somewhere. That wouldn't be quite such a worry if I knew they weren't in a built-up area, but the technical people are worried that the detonators don't have an indefinite life and may degrade. You'd like to think that would mean that they wouldn't go bang, but I'm told it's possible that they'll go bang without being triggered. And on top of that we don't know which particular bunch of nutters have got them.'

'But surely the army have plenty of them too?' Valentin asked.

'You think that's a comfort? The idea that we can stop a bunch of delusional nationalist airheads by sending a bigger bunch of psychotic dandies after them doesn't exactly make me feel that all's right with the world.'

'You're distinctly jaundiced today,' observed Valentin.

'I've got one junior out of touch miles away and the other one is just down the corridor but might as well be miles away as she tries to get to grips with Kuchař's filing system — a task that's probably beyond most human beings — and I'm about to take over the responsibilities of a respected friend and colleague.'

'I thought you were taking over from Lukas?'

'I am.'

'I've never heard you speak like that about him before. Usually you say he's a —'

Slonský cut Valentin off. 'That was before he was leaving. I now realise that I may have been hasty.'

'At least it's gone quiet in the newspapers.'

'Until they hear about the mongrel offspring of a T-34 tank and a big popgun that we've got parked up God knows where.'

'You'll get it sorted out soon.'

'That's just it. If this was crime fiction it would all be wrapped up in a few days. They can solve all sorts in less than an hour on television, even allowing for three commercial breaks. People think that's an accurate representation of police work. They don't realise that the real thing is as slow as treacle much of the time. You send stuff to the labs and you wait. You call for witnesses and you wait. You stake a place out and you wait. And wait, and wait. It's just as well I'm notoriously patient.'

Valentin spluttered and coughed. 'Warn me if you're going to say things like that,' he said. 'My beer went right down my nose when I laughed.'

Slonský ignored the comment. 'Documentaries are no better. They hang around with police for a while then they take out all the boring bits. Police raid a flat, and within fifteen seconds they've found a stash of cocaine inside a mattress. They don't show the hours we spend crawling around in roofspaces.'

'The hours Navrátil spends crawling around in roofspaces, you mean.'

'Efficient use of resources. He's smaller than me, and a bit more nimble.'

Valentin tipped back his glass to drain the last of his beer into his mouth, then smacked his glass down with a finality that suggested he had drunk his fill. 'There must be something positive you can build on?'

'I pin my hopes on Doležal.'

'Jesus Maria! I never expected to hear you say that.'

'I know. I begin to doubt my own sanity. But there are some odd things happening in Holice and he's got some leads to follow up. And Klinger has some concerns about where the money is coming from to build an enormous shopping mall there. He may get results first if only because moving money without leaving some kind of trail is difficult. Give him his due, Klinger is tenacious, and once he gets a sniff of money-related naughtiness he's hard to shake off.'

'You don't think that has anything to do with his obsessive nature?'

'You mean the doorknob thing?'

'Well, germs generally.'

'Granted it's a bit unusual. But I'd rather have colleagues who are weird as hell and as efficient as Klinger than some of the delicate flowers we have around at the moment.'

Valentin did not need to ask the identities of those characterised in this way, because it was a conversation that they had conducted many times before. 'Care for another?' he asked.

'I don't know. How many calories is in one of these things?'

Valentin's jaw dropped involuntarily. 'This is beer we're talking about. An essential part of the Czech diet. Count the calories in other things by all means, but never in beer.' He waved their glasses to attract the waiter. 'Besides,' he added, 'it's a well-known fact that Czech beer contains none.'

Slonský climbed the stairs to his flat. As a result of Valentin's satanic influence he seemed to have drunk rather more beer than he had intended and was feeling internally waterlogged. He also had a growing conviction that people were adding extra stairs to the top flight while he was out nowadays.

He fished out his key and found the keyhole with his fingertips. He must get that landing light bulb replaced some day, he thought, as he had been considering for nearly three years now.

He pushed the door open, flicked on the light, and stood amazed. He had been burgled.

The sense of emptiness was overwhelming. His cosy flat now looked rather bare. He could see the carpet in some places, which was not an improvement, and his snow boots had vanished.

Rapidly sobering up, he decided he must be professional and make a list of the missing items. He had never bothered with insurance, so he would have to make up the loss himself if his things weren't recovered, but he knew that they probably would not be. Perhaps he should ring the technicians and get them to check for fingerprints, though only complete idiots would burgle a flat in Prague without wearing gloves these days. Fortunately complete idiots were over-represented in the list of those who burgled Prague flats so there was still a chance, but he thought making the list was more important in case it wasn't worth all the effort and disturbance of having the technicians snuffling around, not to mention the inevitable embarrassment when word got round the station that Slonský's own place had been turned over.

The old television was still in the corner, but that wasn't exactly the most desirable model, unless you were the curator of a museum. For that matter, he could see the radio on the kitchen counter, but he would not have been too distressed to lose that since it did not work anyway, as devices without batteries generally do not. Edging round the room he discovered that the newspapers that had been on the small table had been folded and placed on the shelf beneath, topped by the paperback book he had been reading.

Slinking into the kitchen he saw that much of his crockery had been lifted, leaving horribly bare worksurfaces, except for a folded piece of paper. A ransom note?

He teased it open with the end of a knife in case it bore fingerprints.

*Josef, I hope I haven't moved things around too much. Your boots are in the cupboard behind the television. Don't flush the toilet until the bleach has done its job. Yours, Věra.*

# Chapter 11

To Slonský's mind there was something curiously uncomfortable about a properly ironed shirt, a sensation enhanced by its rarity. In the normal run of things he saw no point in ironing the sleeves, since he never took his jacket off, but since he now had a sharp crease in his sleeves he had better show them off, he thought, so he hung his jacket on the coat-stand under his hat, and began leafing through the papers on his desk.

Peiperová entered with two cups of coffee and deposited one on the corner of his desk. 'New shirt, sir?' she asked.

'No, Peiperová. No uniform today?'

'The Director doesn't need me today, sir, so I'm released back to you.'

'You look surprisingly happy about that.'

'I'd rather be a detective than a glorified secretary, sir.'

'Don't look a gift horse in the mouth, young lady. When you come back from the Director's Office next year you'll know a lot of people in high places. More to the point, they'll know you. And if he gets the job of Director of Police he may send you back before the year is up, because the current Director has a very efficient personal assistant already.'

'Yes, sir. I've met Monika. She is talking about retiring when he does.'

'Surely she's too young.'

'I think she's the same age as you, sir.'

'As I said, too young.'

Peiperová chose not to respond. Agreement would look like insincere flattery and argument might upset her boss. Instead she sipped her coffee and took out her notebook. 'What do you want me to do today, sir?'

'Ah. Good question. Obviously I didn't know you would be here today so I didn't plan anything. But there are a number of things we need to do. I need to see your new and very temporary boss, the Director of Criminal Police, to get him to give the rear end of someone in Pardubice a good kicking. What's his name again?' Slonský examined several scraps of paper on his desk before triumphantly holding up his pay slip. 'I knew I wrote it down somewhere. Vondra. Captain Vondra. Made a note of that?'

'Yes, sir.'

'We need to drop in on Klinger to see if he has discovered anything about the funding of the new development in Holice, but that's not a high priority because if he had he would have come downstairs to tell me. Or at least pushed a note under my door.'

'New development, sir?'

'Lieutenant Doležal has discovered a plan to build a ridiculously large shopping mall in Holice which the promoters can't possibly afford and Klinger is attempting to find out whose money is behind it.'

'I see. Is this a real shopping mall or just a scheme to collect a lot of money and then run off?'

Slonský took a moment to slurp some of his coffee before replying. 'That's an interesting thought. Doležal has been to the site and says you can see some half-hearted clearance work, but suppose that's just for show? I don't know these things but presumably if you're serious about building you'd hire some of those big diggers and a few bags of cement. Let's go and see if there are any.'

'In Holice, sir? Mightn't that compromise other officers?'

'Lieutenant Doležal is being watched closely so he can't do it easily. Did you have any other officer in mind?'

Peiperová blushed despite her best efforts. 'We're not supposed to see each other. You said so yourself.'

'And I meant it. And no doubt if your paths cross you will both behave in a thoroughly professional manner and pretend you've never met. After all, his safety may depend on it. Now, pack up your things and let's go for a nice day out.'

Navrátil was on the bus to Pardubice. Holice was introducing him to a feeling of claustrophobia that he had not experienced before, and he badly needed a day out himself. Besides, he reasoned, he was supposed to be a normal postgraduate student and surely normal postgraduate students do not study all the time? A couple of hours in a bookshop or doing some sightseeing would recharge his batteries nicely and give him some welcome relief from all that caffeine that was making sleep difficult and causing his ears to buzz.

He cradled his old briefcase as the bus chugged along, having decided that he had better not tempt fate by leaving it unattended again. The false bottom was only a matter of a couple of centimetres, and unless an intruder's curiosity was piqued by the weight of the briefcase when all the papers had been tipped out, it was unlikely to be detected by anyone who had no concrete suspicions that it was there, but it was better not to run the risk. Navrátil had, however, left his draft thesis in full view. Gentle questioning of his landlady had not adduced any evidence of a visitor coming to the house and it was hard to imagine that anyone could have entered unnoticed through the rear windows given how close the other buildings were, but undoubtedly someone had been in his room and he could hardly imagine his landlady crawling around under his bed.

After breakfast he had taken a closer look at the back door. It had a very basic lock and it would not have been difficult to pick it, he thought, even if it had been locked; and since it was presently unlocked, and seemed to be so most of the day, all the intruder needed to do was to ensure that the landlady was not in the kitchen when he slipped in.

The bus driver was calling his stop, so Navrátil sprang from his seat and made his way to the door. There was a bus a little after five o'clock that he would catch for the return journey. But first, a little rest and recreation amongst the bright lights of Pardubice was called for.


'Wednesday the thirteenth?' bellowed Slonský. 'Wednesday the thirteenth?'

'Yes, sir,' Peiperová replied quietly. She had not been looking forward to explaining the Director's plan but thought that Slonský should know what lay in store for him at the earliest opportunity.

'Why Wednesday? And why the thirteenth? Is somebody superstitious?'

'The Director wants to be there in person to say goodbye to Captain Lukas and he's on holiday in the last week of June. He didn't have many free evenings in his diary. So he asked me to ensure that you were free so that he could formally bestow your captaincy at the retirement party.'

'I see. And where is this shindig taking place?'

'I've booked the main conference room.'

'No expense spared, then.'

'It's the Captain's retirement after forty years. You can't just say goodbye in a bar.'

'Well, that's what I'd want.'

'But what matters is what Captain Lukas would want, sir.'

Slonský's wrath subsided. 'I can't argue with that. It would make his wife and daughters happy, and if they're happy he'll be ecstatic. So I've got less than two weeks to get my uniform alterations done.'

'The Director has received assurances that your uniform will be ready tomorrow, sir.'

'The Director? Or the Director's Personal Assistant?'

'He asked me to make the call, sir.'

'Anything else you've taken care of that you might like to tell me about?'

Peiperová, who was normally confident, bit her lower lip uncertainly.

'Spit it out, lass.'

'The Director wants me to tell you that Mrs Slonská would be welcome too.'

'Not by me she bloody wouldn't!'

'It's a family occasion, sir, so the Director thought…'

'She's not family. She opted out of being family when she ran off with that slimy leather-jacketed so-called poet over thirty years ago. And how, pray, does the Director know of the existence of my estranged wife?'

'I was asked a direct question, sir.'

'And you couldn't lie?'

'No, sir.'

'So you told the Director I had a wife.'

'Yes, sir. I did say that I wasn't sure what the current state of your relationship was…'

'Relationship? We don't have a relationship. Occasionally she comes round and cooks me a meal. Then she goes home. She sweeps the floor and cleans the worktops.'

'Yes, sir.'

'And do you know why she does that?'

'No, sir.'

'Neither do I, and it bugs me.'

'Should I drive, sir?'

'No, I can drive and shout at the same time. You're a woman, Peiperová. What, if anything, is going through her head?'

'We're not all the same, sir. I can't presume to know what Mrs Slonská is thinking.'

'No, I…'

'But since you asked me,' Peiperová quickly continued, in case the licence to give relationship advice were about to be withdrawn, 'I'd say it's guilt.'

'Guilt?'

'Guilt, sir. Women do guilt very well. At least, women of that vintage do.'

'I've seen no sign of it before.'

'With respect, sir, you don't expect to see it, so you don't see it. But she feels guilty about the way things turned out.'

'And your evidence for this is?'

Peiperová was warming to her theme and turned in her seat to allow herself to engage better. 'Sir, when you got married you'll have had ideas about what the future would be like. Maybe you don't know what's going to happen over the next ten years, just as Jan and I don't know exactly. We have plans, of course, but we don't know if they'll work out the way we expect. But by the time you're nearing sixty, everybody's plans look much the same. If you've had children, they've left to start their own lives, so the two of you are left to grow old together and be a support to one another.'

Slonský opened his mouth but was silenced abruptly.

'Please let me finish, sir! So if you see life as a journey, there was a station on the way that you'd get to about now, and you wouldn't want to make the rest of life's journey on your own. It's just that you and Mrs Slonská have finished up going along different routes to arrive at this stop. But she is trying to make amends and get back together so that the two of you won't be lonely in your old age. She wants your company, sir.'

'My company? Nobody wants my company, lass. Valentin spends more time with me than anyone else but that's only because I buy most of the drinks.'

'Forgive me, sir, but you're wrong. She's doing these things for you as a sort of penance.'

'I thought Navrátil was the one who was big on penance.'

'He is, sir. Really big.'

'So why are you doing his work?'

'We've talked about it, sir. I'm sorry, it's none of our business.'

'And what conclusion did you and Romeo come up with?'

'That you're wounded, and rightly so, but that you deserve some companionship in your retirement, and nobody would suit you better than your wife.'

There followed an awkward silence that lasted about five kilometres.

'I'm sorry, sir, I've overstepped the mark.'

'Yes, you have.'

'I didn't mean to interfere in your private life. Jan and I just want you to have the happiness we have.'

'I know. I will think about what you've said. But for now we have some murderers to catch, so could we please give our undivided attention to that?'

Slonský had decided that a coffee would be the first matter

requiring attention once they reached Holice, and immediately headed for the most visible café, which happened to be the one that Navrátil favoured. He and Peiperová placed their order at the counter.

'Sit anywhere you like and I'll bring them over. If you don't mind, there's a young student who usually sits at the table by the electricity socket. He's not in yet but he'll probably show up soon.'

Peiperová began to speak but Slonský got in first. 'What's he a student of?'

'I don't know exactly. He's doing a questionnaire about being Czech.'

'We'll look out for him,' Slonský replied with a smile. 'It sounds like fun.'

They took their seats and Slonský opened a map he had obtained through Mucha. Goodness knows where Mucha got it, but there must be a store of maps somewhere at headquarters.

'Doležal says they're evicting people from these cottages here. We'll drive over there after coffee to take a look around.'

'What are we looking for, sir?'

'Anything that shouldn't be there. I think he's probably on the right track when he says that crime money is behind this. It's a way of laundering a stash. But there's just a possibility that there's something on the site that Veselý wants to get hold of without drawing attention to it — a mine, for example. We'll probably find it's fenced off but I've got some opera glasses in my pocket.'

'You like the opera, sir?'

'Don't sound so incredulous, Peiperová. No, I didn't say I like opera. But I like opera glasses. They fit my coat pocket nicely.'

The café owner brought the coffees and waited for Slonský to move the map so she could place them on the table. When he showed no signs of doing so she stood with them in her hands. 'Where would you like me to put these?'

'Anywhere you like except where my finger is,' Slonský replied.

'Planning an outing?' she asked.

'No, we're here to inspect the site of the new shopping mall. I hear it's going to be quite something.'

The owner snorted. 'If it ever gets built.'

'You're doubtful?'

'Look, it's one of Veselý's schemes, isn't it? I was at school with him. He was always full of big ideas.'

'He's going to need a lot of money to build this one. Done well since he left school, has he?' Slonský asked.

'He's comfortable. He's built a few houses here and there and got himself made deputy mayor. But if he's got this kind of money why does his wife do her own hair?'

'That's a good point. These cottages here — what's going to happen to the old people there?'

'The cottages? Why should they have to move?'

'Well, the plans call for the hotel and the old people's flats to be built across there.'

The woman was indignant. 'That's the first I've heard of it. The story in the newspaper only mentioned a mall. There was nothing about hotels or moving people out.'

Slonský rummaged in his pockets until he found a photocopy and opened it out. 'There you are. Shopping mall, cinema, hotel, restaurants, flats.'

She snatched it up and examined it closely. 'We'll see about that. My aunt lives in one of those cottages.' She eyed him suspiciously. 'You're not an investor, are you?'

'Madam, do I look like I've got cash to throw at a white elephant?'

'No, but you read about eccentric millionaires who wear the same coat for years.'

Peiperová coughed as she tried to deal with the coffee that had somehow found its way into her nose.

'You must forgive my assistant,' Slonský remarked. 'She's going to another job next week and she's demob happy.'

'Well, if you're not an investor, what's your interest in all this?' the owner asked. Slonský flashed his badge. 'Goodness, the place is crawling with new police lately!'

Slonský hoped that Navrátil had not been rumbled. 'How do you mean?'

'Well, the other day there was a new one in here. Thin chap, dark haired, thinning on top, moustache.'

'Face like a bloodhound?'

'That'll be him.'

'One of our team. He's filling in for poor Lieutenant Sedlák.'

'That was a real shame. Sedlák was a good sort.'

'Did you know the others who died?'

'I didn't know the one who ran it all. But the Lackos used to come in now and again. Jakub was good with his hands. He could fix almost anything. His son wasn't able to help much.'

'Following in his father's footsteps?'

'No, Pavel was a bit odd. He worked for his dad because he couldn't get a job anywhere else. He had Down's Syndrome. Lovely boy, never any trouble. Followed his dad everywhere. In a way it's a blessing he died in the accident. He'd have been lost if he'd survived and his dad hadn't.'

Slonský could feel a rage surging inside him. 'Thank you,' he said. 'I didn't know that.'

The door chimed as someone entered and the owner went off to attend to the new customer.

'That's horrible,' Peiperová commented.

'Yes, it is. The only good thing is that perhaps he was too confused to be frightened when they sat them down in a circle.'

'We've got to find them, sir. This can't go unpunished.'

'No crime goes unpunished on my watch, Peiperová. This one least of all. Come on, drink up and we'll go and see what we can find.'


Slonský dialled a number on his mobile phone. 'We're in town,' he said. 'Have you got a few minutes?'

'Where are you?' asked Doležal.

'Outside the café that Navrátil uses.'

'I know the one. I can be there in twenty minutes.'

'Don't come here. Meet us near the cottages.'

'Will do.'

Slonský told Peiperová to start driving and gave her some approximate directions before dialling another number.

'Klinger speaking.'

'Slonský here. How are you getting on with tracking the money behind the Central Czech Shopping Plaza?'

'Nothing I'd take to court yet, but the indications are that we'll be doing some bear hunting.'

'It's Russian money?'

'So my informants believe. There's no point in asking the Russian police to confirm the names — someone will just tip them off — but I know at least two of them. They run some clubs in Prague.'

'I take it these are not flower arranging clubs?'

'Not unless flower arranging is considerably more lucrative than I've been led to believe.'

'So how did Veselý get in touch with them?'

'That remains to be discovered. We could, conceivably, question him, but I think that could be hazardous for him.'

'It'll certainly be hazardous if I discover he's complicit in the murder of a boy with Down's Syndrome.'

'I didn't know that. And I shall, on this occasion, volunteer to hold your jacket while you question him. But I meant that these Russians are not cuddly bears. If they're up to something and they think that he may disclose their secrets his life expectancy could be substantially reduced.'

'You're probably right. I'll leave him alone for a minute, then. That doesn't mean that you have to.'


Doležal glanced around nervously as he climbed out of the car.

'Expecting trouble?' asked Slonský.

'I don't know who to trust here,' Doležal answered.

'Just like Prague, then. So help us to get our bearings.'

Doležal ran a finger along the map. 'That's the line of the fence to our right. Behind the fence are the cottages I was talking about.'

'Where the old lady lives who knows nothing about this. As well as the aunt of the woman who runs the café, who may, of course, be the same woman you've met. Why do I get a really bad feeling about all of this?' Slonský asked.

'But what does it have to do with the explosion, sir?' Peiperová added. 'That's the crime we're meant to be investigating.'

'We don't know that the mall project, misguided as it is, has anything illegal about it. And, if it has, we don't know that there's any connection at all to the killings,' Doležal agreed.

Slonský stood scratching his hip as he looked hard at the rusting fence. 'The trouble is,' he opined, 'that when you're faced with a foul stench you don't bother about whether it's one foul stench or two. You sort out what you can and then see if it smells any better.'

'Meaning?' Doležal replied.

'Meaning that I don't know what I'm talking about,' Slonský answered. 'By which I don't mean that I'm talking rubbish, but that I don't know enough to know whether I'm talking rubbish or not.' He walked over and rattled the fence.

'You don't need to do that,' Doležal told him. 'It's not there to keep us out, just to mark the boundary. You can walk round it.'

'I know. But why is the boundary so important that they put up a fence? It's only going to get in the way when they clear the site. Was anyone going to dispute their ownership?'

'Maybe it's about the bits they don't own,' suggested Peiperová. 'Perhaps they don't yet have the whole site.'

Slonský became surprisingly animated. 'Write that thought down somewhere! I think you're on to something.' He clambered through the undergrowth to the top of the short rise and looked across the site, before bounding back down to join them. 'Their best chance of getting the parcels of land at a good price is if each seller doesn't know they need them all, so I can understand why they've kept it as secret as they can. Veselý wants investors, so he has to talk about the scale of the thing, but to the locals it's being kept firmly under wraps. The council has agreed the land deal but there hasn't been anything I've found in the local press that would let people know it had happened, which is strange considering the number of articles, photos and interviews the council managed to milk out of getting funding for a new wing on the school. Of course, if you become aware that you own the last parcel of land they need your price for letting it go will go through the roof.'

'Except that if it's bear money they'd send some men to persuade you to sell,' interrupted Doležal.

'Is it possible the four men owned some land here that they wouldn't sell so this is a warning to others?' Peiperová chipped in.

'The problem with the notion that it's a secret message is that others have to know what the message means, or there's no point in sending it,' Slonský answered. 'If I send you a couple of fish it's just a supper unless you know it's a warning that you're going to be taking a swim in concrete flippers.'

'Everyone is so damn secretive,' complained Doležal. 'It's as if they're all guilty of something. The police are making no effort to find out who killed these men, and they're making no progress trying to find that gun. We gave them a good lead or two, so it makes you think they aren't really trying.'

'I agree,' said Slonský. 'The whole thing smells worse than my walking boots. Let's hope Navrátil is getting somewhere.'

Navrátil, at that precise moment, was getting a hazelnut pancake and a cappuccino. He had been giving some thought to what the café owner could have meant when she told him to watch out for the police. It cannot have been a warning about Doležal, because she had only just set eyes on him for the first time. It must have been about the police in general; and yet there were no signs that she was anything other than a respectable small businesswoman with no particular reason to be wary of his colleagues. So what was it about the local police that gave her cause for concern? What was it that he was doing that meant he needed to be careful? He was masquerading as a postgraduate student of politics, with rather right-wing views.

What was there in that which might bring him some grief? Presumably the right-wing views, though he had said nothing untoward. So were the police on the look-out for right-wingers? Had there been some other incidents that had not been reported to Prague? Perhaps there was more to this than met the eye.

Slonský had decided to detour to Pardubice to pay a courtesy call on Captain Vondra. Ostensibly its purpose was to brief Vondra on progress to date on a crime which had, after all, happened on his patch, but since Slonský did not trust Vondra and had no intention of sharing any useful information, the interview was rather stilted.

'How is Lieutenant Doležal settling in?' Slonský asked breezily.

'Early days yet,' Vondra responded.

'He's a good man.'

'I'm sure he is.'

'Diligent. Tenacious,' Slonský added.

'Good qualities in a policeman.'

'Forgive me, but you sound guarded.'

'No,' Vondra replied. 'It's just that he has two bosses and in my experience that rarely works well.'

'Only for this investigation. Once we wrap this up he's entirely yours,' Slonský answered. 'Think what would have happened if Sedlák had survived. You would have asked Prague for support and he would have been detached to work with me. No difference.'

'I suppose so,' Vondra conceded. 'Except that, of course, I would already know Sedlák.'

'That's true. I'd have been the one having to make up my mind about him. Have you made any headway on the search for the gun?'

'Not really. The trouble is that on the evening of Liberation Day quite a few people who might have been witnesses were in no state to give a statement. We put out a story locally that we were keen to track down the driver of a military vehicle who might be a witness to an accident, so if anyone could give us details of any military vehicles that had been in the area they could ring in and we could track the driver down.'

'Very enterprising. Did it work?'

'You wouldn't believe how many military vehicles there were driving around on Liberation Day,' Vondra moaned. 'But nobody mentioned a big gun.'

Slonský was unsurprised. The attitude of many of his countrymen was that they did not want interference in their lives, so they would not interfere in others', and if people want to drive around the country in self-propelled artillery then we should let them do so as long as they were not frightening pets.

'Tell me,' he asked as if changing the subject, 'do you know Veselý well?'

'The deputy mayor at Holice? Not well, but I know him a bit, obviously. He comes to some of our public safety meetings.'

'What do you make of him?'

'Well turned out. Always wearing a good suit and usually has a bit of a tan. Shakes a lot of hands and asks a few questions. But I'll tell you one thing — it always seems to me that he's representing Veselý rather than the people of Holice.'

'You think he's in politics for what he can get out of it?' Slonský asked.

'Aren't they all? But him more than most, I'd say.'

'And the mayor doesn't mind?'

'Nerad? He was on the make himself for years, if you ask me. But he doesn't have the clout to deal with Vesely. I reckon that they've probably got a sort of arrangement.'

'What sort of arrangement?'

'I think Nerad tolerates Vesely so long as he can keep the title of mayor,' Vondra explained. 'And Vesely doesn't want all the work and restrictions that come with being mayor so long as he can get the advantages. This way he goes to what he wants to go to and doesn't have to eat a load of cheap chicken lunches. Being deputy suits him fine.'

'So where do you think he's getting the money for this development of his?'

Vondra sighed deeply as if it were a stupid question. 'There is no money. There will be no development. It's just pie in the sky. Still, it keeps him off the streets, I suppose.'

'You reckon?'

'We've seen it before. He comes up with a plan, it doesn't fly and he blames someone else. But while it's being discussed, he's in the news every day.'

Slonsky was unconvinced. 'He seems to have spent plenty getting this one off the ground. Brochures, models, videos and fences. He's even started clearing some of the ground.'

'He'd need to do that to keep the investors interested. Who knows, one day he'll get all the cash he needs and we'll wake up to find we've got a bowling alley and a cinema.' Vondra yawned expansively. 'But I wouldn't hold your breath,' he added.


Navrátil had been dozing gently on the warm bus back to Holice when he thought he saw Peiperová and Slonsky driving in the opposite direction. It was a fleeting glimpse, and he might well have been dreaming if he had nodded off, but it occurred to him that they would not have come to visit him if there was any risk of compromising his cover, and in a little town like Holice where outsiders stuck out that risk would have been considerable.

He changed his shirt and set out for the bar as usual. He was engaged in the arduous task of compiling a list of his friends and relatives who would expect an invitation to his wedding when he became aware that someone had taken the seat opposite. He found himself looking at a young man with dark hair, a pleasant smile and an effortlessly superior manner.

'I'm sorry, I was engrossed in something else,' Navrátil stammered.

'So I could see. My friends tell me that you're doing some amusing research.'

Navrátil explained the purpose of his questionnaire and offered one to the newcomer.

'Of course. Do you have a pen?'

The young man began ticking boxes without, it seemed, much need to think about the answers. 'I hear that your supervisor has been critical,' he smiled.

Navrátil was not aware that he had said that to anyone in town. Was it possible that this young man was connected to the intrusion in his room?

'That's right. He is fervently pro-EU. I take a different view.'

'So do I, and there are many others who think as we do. Not that there is anything anti-Western about us, you understand. We merely worry that our special Czech heritage is being undervalued.'

'I couldn't agree more,' Navrátil replied.

The young man held out his hand. 'I'm sorry, I have the advantage of you, Mr Ondráček.' Seeing the surprise on Navrátil's face, he pointed to the battered thesis on the table top. 'It's on the front cover. I assume that is your thesis, and you're not carrying someone else's around.'

Navrátil relaxed. 'No, it is mine. I'd forgotten it was there.'

'Better not lose it. A lot of work must have gone into that.'

'I have a file copy back in Prague,' Navrátil responded, hoping that it was true and that Poznar could produce another one if this folder were to go missing.

'I'm David Nerad.'

'Are you related to the mayor?'

'My uncle. My father is his older brother.'

'Does your uncle share your views?'

David laughed. 'My uncle has no views. That is why he is a successful politician here. He is very good at giving the impression that he agrees with whoever spoke to him last. But he loves this town, and he'll oppose anything that might damage its future.'

'You think the EU will damage it?'

'Not particularly, though the idea that the West is the land of milk and honey means that our best young people are seduced away. They go to work in London and come back to tell their friends that they can earn more cleaning toilets in England than they can earn as a skilled worker here.'

'Isn't that true?'

'It may be true, but the important thing is that you're still cleaning toilets. Czechs have a more important role in the world than that.'

Navrátil found himself saying agreeing.

'Perhaps you might be interested in meeting a few like-minded people I know. We're meeting on Saturday morning for a discussion. I'm sure they'd be fascinated to hear about your research, if you felt able to share a little?'

'That would be good. Perhaps they'll complete some of my questionnaires too.'

'I'm sure they will,' David Nerad smiled. 'But they may give surprisingly unanimous views. Shall I meet you here at half past nine and then we'll walk to the meeting room? It's only a few steps.'

'I'd be delighted,' Navrátil answered.

They shook hands, and Nerad wished him luck. Navrátil had a feeling that he had just made the contact he had been hoping for. Progress, at last! But now he had to read and learn "his" thesis so he could speak sensibly on the matter on Saturday morning.

# Chapter 12

Navrátil sighed with disappointment. Now that he had to read the mocked-up thesis closely he realised that Poznar's department had simply cut and pasted sections from a range of sources without any attempt to smooth over the joins or remove incongruities. For example, on page twelve there was reference to the outcome of a meeting that was described on page thirty-five as something that had not yet happened. Two different men were described as the current Prime Minister. Admittedly Prime Ministers came and went with shocking regularity, but the Czech Republic had not yet thought of appointing them in pairs.

He had asked for a copy of the thesis on a memory stick, largely because he thought it would be more convincing if he were seen to be working on one, so he plugged it into his laptop and begin editing the thesis to make it more presentable. It took him most of the next day but by the end of it he had a version which read much better. It was still plagiarized nonsense, but at least it was stylistically more polished plagiarized nonsense.

He paced his room rehearsing some of the facts and figures and selected some quotes from a range of people that he thought might seem to be supporting his argument. An internet search produced some interviews with a number of unappealing individuals with frankly unpleasant views, but he felt he could adopt and adapt them to make them seem more acceptable to the mainstream, and a further search produced videos of some speeches that might inform his performance and improve his public speaking technique.

No method actor ever prepared more thoroughly than Navrátil did for his role as Michal Ondráček.

Slonský was bewildered. Such a thing had never happened to him before, and it was deeply, deeply disquieting.

On his arrival in Prague he had dropped into the gym to check his weight and had discovered that he had already lost five kilos. Well, 4.6 if precision were called for, but that was nearer to five than four.

Flushed with achievement, he had decided he could afford to reward himself with the mixed grill at a little basement restaurant he knew, the platter consisting of a substantial portion of every kind of edible animal and a mound of sauerkraut.

And he could not eat it all.

He paused to let some go down. He tried drinking half a litre of premium beer. Neither did the trick. There was no doubt about it. He was full.

He paid his bill and stomped to the bar where a disgustingly trim looking Valentin was reading a newspaper while sipping a glass of water.

'That's not the paper you write for,' said Slonský accusingly. 'Are you pinching a story for tomorrow's issue?'

'My story is filed,' replied Valentin with dignity. 'Top of page two, since you ask. And why are you behaving like a boar with his snout in a trap?'

'I'm not. Just a bit of indigestion, that's all.'

Valentin squinted at him. 'I can see you've lost some weight.'

'Five kilos. Not bad for two weeks.'

'Three weeks,' Valentin corrected him.

'Three very stressful weeks. In case you hadn't noticed I've got a quadruple murder to solve.'

'I wasn't going to ask about that, since it obviously isn't going too well.'

'How do you mean?'

'If you'd arrested someone you'd have tipped off your best and oldest mate. Like you promised,' Valentin added with emphasis.

'That doesn't mean we're not making progress.'

'Out of respect for confidentiality I won't ask how Navrátil is getting on, but how is Doležal doing?'

'He's frustrated. His colleagues don't seem to be trying too hard to clear this up.'

'Isn't that just the provincial way? Let the big shots from Prague do it and if they fail we'll just giggle behind our hands.'

'There's always an element of that, but there's more to it. Look, have you got your notebook with you?'

Valentin produced it from his pocket and licked the tip of his pencil. 'Never go anywhere without it. Speak on.'

'The local head of crime is a man called Vondra. Captain Vondra — don't know his first name. I want to know if there's anything at all that I can use to get some leverage with him. I don't care if it's a parking ticket in 1990. There's probably nothing in your files, but just in case, would you take a look? The same goes for the deputy mayor of Holice, a man called Veselý. He's setting up a big property deal to build an enormous shopping and housing complex on land he's got cheap from the local council, but we don't know how he's funding it. Just between us there's a chance that it's Russian money, but we need to find out how he came to the Russians' attention. There has to be a link of some kind, someone who acted as a go-between. Anything you can find would be appreciated.'

'Forgive me for pointing this out, but if you're looking for criminality, wouldn't the police records be a better bet?'

'I'll look in there first thing tomorrow. Or I'll get Mucha to do it, which is pretty much the same thing. But if the link I'm looking for was criminal, we'd have banged him up, so I don't think it is.'

'And is this connected to the explosion?'

Slonský took a long pull of his beer before answering. 'If it isn't, it's quite a coincidence that both are going on in a tiny place at the same time. But I have no idea how they could be linked. The explosion was nowhere near the site of the development. After all, you'd want a shopping mall near the main road where plenty of people are going past, whereas if you want a thumping big gun to go unnoticed you'd put it somewhere that people don't normally go. The only thing that I can think of is that Veselý is somehow mixed up in both. Except that I've met him, and he's a blabbermouth. You can't imagine him keeping a secret for forty days, let alone forty years, and he can't have been more than seven or eight when the Russians came.'

Valentin closed his book. 'I'll let you know if I find anything. Now, you're off duty. Will you have another?'

'No, I'm full, thanks.'

Valentin immediately clapped his palm to Slonský's forehead. 'Are you sickening for something?'

'No, just had a big dinner. I think I'll get an early night.'

Valentin's jaw dropped involuntarily. 'It's not even eleven o'clock.'

'Busy day tomorrow. I've got to get Mucha going on those records, remember?'

Sergeant Mucha listened intently to the request. 'I thought you said you had a job for me?' he said. 'That's singular. You know — one job. So far you've given me three.'

'All part of the same enquiry though.'

'But three jobs.'

Slonský shrugged. 'It all depends how you look at it. Think of it like the Holy Trinity — three in one, one in three, indivisible.'

'I'm not religious. To me, three jobs is three jobs.'

'So what do you want?'

Mucha lowered his voice. 'It's like this. Next Tuesday I'm off duty. But now the wife's sister has announced she's coming up to Prague for the day.'

'The Evil Witch of Kutná Hora?'

'That's the one. So I could do with needing to be somewhere. Somewhere I can't put off.'

'Next Tuesday, you say? I can think of two ways your services could be absolutely indispensable. It's the day before Captain Lukas' retirement do, so you could help Peiperová do whatever it is she thinks needs to be done to make the place look festive. Or, given that she will be working for the Director of Criminal Police by then, and Navrátil is off on a jolly of his own somewhere, you could assist me in a lightning raid on suspicious premises.'

'Where are you planning to raid next Tuesday?'

'I haven't decided yet. Probably a bar or two. I'm sure we can find somebody who needs following. We can improvise something on the day.'

'Will it be dangerous?'

'How can you ask me such a thing? Would I lead my best mate in the police force into any kind of danger?'

'Yes. You've done it before.'

'Okay, but never knowingly. And if you're talking about that warehouse raid all those years ago, remember I was the one who took the bullet.'

'The ricochet.'

'Exactly. I was not running away.'

'I testified as much when they tried to bill you for the replacement trousers.'

'So you did. Do we have an understanding?'

Mucha summoned another officer to stand by the Visitor Register. 'I can't stand here yapping all day,' he told Slonský. 'I've got three jobs to do.'

Slonský was taking the stairs slowly, given that he had a pastry balanced on top of his coffee cup, when he heard a strange snuffling noise coming from his office. He toyed with the idea of drawing his gun but that meant he would have had to put his breakfast down somewhere first, so he tiptoed towards his door and nudged it with his foot.

Peiperová was clearing her desk, putting the contents of the drawer into a plastic carrier bag and wiping a tear from her cheek as she did so.

'What's all this about?' asked Slonský.

Peiperová snapped to attention. 'Sorry, sir, I didn't hear you come in.'

'Full marks for the tidy uniform and the stance, but if you come to attention in front of me again I may throw this coffee down your front. We don't do that in this office.'

'No, sir. It's one of the things I'll miss.'

'I wouldn't be much of a detective if I didn't detect some tears.'

Peiperová fought unsuccessfully to hold them in. 'I'm sorry, sir. Not at my best today. I wonder if I'm doing the right thing.'

'Sit down and let's have a chat.'

The young policewoman did as instructed, using a tissue to wipe her face. 'Sorry, sir, this isn't me.'

'Well, if it isn't you it's a damn good impersonation. It had me fooled.'

'I mean the crying bit. I hate you seeing me like that.'

'This is not goodbye, Peiperová. It's just farewell. If I thought for a minute you weren't coming back I'd be crying too, and neither of us would like that.'

Peiperová forced a smile. 'No, sir.'

'The way I look at it, the Director of Criminal Police is my boss. If he says he wants you for a year, I can't really refuse him. If he's my boss he's also your boss, so you can't really refuse him either. So this is not a choice you've made. It's an instruction you've fallen in with. Therefore, there is no question of doing the right thing or the wrong thing. You're just doing a thing.'

'Yes, sir.'

'You will excel there just like you've excelled here. My only fear is that you'll be promoted to captain and sent somewhere as my equivalent.'

'Hardly likely, sir. I'm not even a lieutenant yet.'

'I knew a man once who went from new recruit to captain inside a fortnight. Mind, his dad was a member of the Communist Party Presidium.'

'Those days have gone, sir.'

'Yes, they have. And it's our job to keep them gone.' He stood up and walked to Peiperová's desk. 'It was a bit of a squeeze to get this in here thirteen months ago. Navrátil and

Mucha had to move that heavy filing cabinet and turn it sideways. It wore me out just watching them. But even though we could do with the space, this desk is going nowhere. It'll be here for you when you get back.'

'Won't you be moving into the captain's office, sir?'

'I'll have two desks. And, in time, I hope to perfect the art of not being at the one everybody expects. We're a team, lass, and this is our spiritual home.'

'Yes, sir. I feel better now, sir.' She sprang to her feet and extended her hand. 'Thank you for everything, sir. I've really enjoyed it and I'm so grateful for the opportunity.'

'The last year has passed very quickly. I hope the next one goes by even faster, for both of us.'

They shook hands.

'Oh, one thing, sir. I found this key taped to the side of my desk drawer. Any idea whose it is?'

'Ah! I've been looking for that. I'll take charge of it for you.'

Mucha passed over a sheaf of printout. 'Vondra's personnel file.'

'How did you get hold of that so quickly?'

'Well, would you believe he's applied for a job here as night shift sergeant on the front desk?'

'Has he really? Must be bored with being a captain, I suppose.'

'I guess. Anyway, once he applies for a job, his future boss can inspect his personnel record, so I did.'

'Well, let's see what we've got.' Slonský browsed the pages slowly. 'My God, what a boring life he's led.'

'I thought that too.'

'It's not exactly a page-turner, is it? I can't see it being made into a blockbuster film.'

'It's short of disciplinary stuff too. A couple of late arrivals on shift, a reminder to keep his political views to himself and not allow them to creep into reports, and a stroppy note from the police sports club about not paying his subs on time.'

'Does it tell us what those political views were?' Slonský asked.

'I don't think so. It's come from the local Director of Police, so it was obviously escalated to him because Vondra was only a lieutenant at the time.'

'That's more than saying the local mayor is a moron, then.'

'Unless he said it to the mayor,' Mucha replied. 'But we'll never know, because the original report isn't attached.'

'Thanks for this lot. Anything else?'

Mucha took out his notebook and found the most recent entries. 'Veselý has never been to Russia, so far as I can tell. He has a passport but it's only been logged at the border once since 1989, when he went to Poland as part of a trade mission two years ago. Strictly the invitation went to the mayor, but Veselý went instead. No criminal offences and his taxes are up to date.'

'That's suspicious in its own right. I can't remember when a politician was good at paying taxes.'

'Maybe he isn't crooked. Maybe he's just hopelessly optimistic. Perhaps he really believes this development will be the making of him.'

'The snag with that hypothesis is that if he isn't crooked I don't have any other ideas. Forensics isn't giving me much except that the murderer was probably injured himself in the blast, but nobody seems to have turned up at a hospital or clinic with wounds consistent with being hit by grenade fragments.'

'Or nobody is telling you.'

'Or telling Doležal. But why didn't the local police do that once we told them?'

'They'd lost their local crime officer.'

'They'd lost the crime officer at a small station. The next tier up at Pardubice should have flooded them with help, but there's been nothing. Sedlák was one of our own. He deserved better than he's getting from his colleagues.'

'It's almost as if they don't want the murderer caught,' said Mucha.

'But why? It isn't as if they didn't like Sedlák, and it's not as if there's any suggestion that any of them were involved in the murder.'

'Maybe they just want to make us in Prague look bad,' Mucha suggested.

'We don't need their help for that.'

Veselý threw open the door and advanced with a smile and an outstretched hand.

'Mr Klinger!'

'It's Major Klinger actually,' said Klinger, producing his police identity card. 'Fraud Squad.'

The fake smile froze within the fake tan of Veselý's face. 'I see. Well, you'd better come in. Žofie, no interruptions, please.'

The bemused secretary nodded her agreement and returned to her computer wondering how much longer she would have a job.

Klinger walked over to the wall, polishing his spectacles as he inspected the plan of the proposed development.

'This is very … ambitious,' he commented. 'Progressive. Forward thinking.'

'I like to think so,' Veselý agreed.

'The scale of the project is considerable.'

'Yes. It will be the biggest development of its kind outside Prague, I understand.'

Klinger puffed on his glasses and gave the lens a further polish. 'In a town which currently boasts a few small shops and a fairly ramshackle apology for a supermarket.'

'Obviously the intended clientele is not confined to Holice,' Veselý responded. 'We anticipate that it will attract people from far away. We plan to run subsidised courtesy buses from Prague.'

'Very enterprising. And I see there will be people living on site.'

'Sheltered housing. It's in short supply in Prague, and very expensive. I'm told we should have no trouble filling it very quickly.'

'And a cinema?'

'Leisure complex,' Veselý corrected him. 'There'll be a tenpin bowling alley too.'

Klinger smiled, though Klinger's smiles were often unnerving to those who experienced them. 'Is tenpin bowling popular amongst the elderly, then?' he asked.

'Not really,' Veselý answered, feeling that a response of some kind was expected, however inadequate.

'Well, it's your money. Actually, let's look into that a little. You keep saying "we". Who are "we"?'

'We? My investors and myself.'

'And your investors are?'

'Am I obliged to answer?'

'No. Not yet. You may become so, but you are not obliged to answer during an informal interview. However, I have made enquiries, as I am entitled to do, and I have compiled a statement of your known personal assets.'

Klinger dusted the chair with his handkerchief and sat down before passing a photocopy over the desk. 'On the face of it, no reputable bank would advance you the sum necessary to complete this project. In fact, you could barely raise the cash for the bowling alley. It follows that your investors must be bearing the bulk of the costs. I am interested in where that money comes from. I need hardly remind you that if it is found to be the proceeds of crime that would place you in a very difficult position.'

'I'm sure that they are all above board,' Veselý protested.

'Did you know them before beginning this project?'

'Not exactly.'

'What do you mean, "not exactly"? Surely the only possible answers are yes and no.'

'No, then.'

'Did they approach you, or did you go to them?'

'We met at a trade fair. I was trying to promote this region as an attractive option for foreign investment.'

'I must congratulate you. You seem to have done it very well. But — you will forgive the observation, I'm sure — if you were there in an official capacity as deputy mayor, it seems inappropriate to enter into any private financial undertakings.'

'They made the suggestion. I was able to persuade the regional council to make some land available in lieu of a cash investment. But our partners were very keen that we should illustrate our full commitment by making an investment ourselves.'

Klinger smiled his thin smile again. Veselý wiped his sweaty hands on his desk blotter.

'Yes, I can see how that might happen,' said Klinger. 'Your partners, I believe, are Russian.'

'Yes.'

'Was their money already within the Czech Republic or did they transfer it?'

'I'm … I'm not sure.'

'And what line of business are they in?'

'Entertainment. And, obviously, property development.'

'Yet, despite their expertise, and your lack of it, you're the one at the front.'

'I'm not a complete beginner,' Veselý objected. 'I've built developments before.'

'Indeed you have,' agreed Klinger, drawing two sheets from his briefcase. 'A pair of four-storey blocks of flats, and a plumbing warehouse.'

'Everyone has to start somewhere.'

'I suppose they must. And, plainly, you are very familiar with the district. You know some influential people.'

'What the hell is that meant to mean? I haven't paid any bribes if that's what you're hinting.'

'How could you?' agreed Klinger. 'You don't have the money. Your partners could, of course.'

'I know nothing about that.'

'Well, we'll leave that for now. I have discovered that you have taken out a loan from a bank in Pardubice. It appears to be on normal commercial terms.'

'That's right.'

'It also appears to be for around four and a half million euros. I am informed that this project is likely to cost about six times that amount.'

Veselý swallowed hard. 'Not quite that much.'

'And if my information is correct, your partners have committed around seventeen and a half million.'

Veselý ran his finger around the inside of his collar. 'About that.'

Klinger smiled once again. 'Then there remains a shortfall. Unless there are other investors of whom I have no knowledge?'

'A number of local people have made money available. Obviously their investments are small, but added together…'

'Yes, the power of co-operative action. Added together … what? Three million?'

'Nearer two.'

'So there is a deficiency?'

'At this moment in time. But investments are still being sought. I have every confidence that…'

'And have the Russians paid in full?'

'We don't need the full investment just yet.'

'No, you don't. But I've seen the project's bank account. The Russians appear to have handed over about five million euros just a few days ago, and that's it. How confident are you that they are able to deliver their full investment?'

'Why wouldn't they? They'd lose more than I would.'

'They would, wouldn't they? Because you don't actually have the money you've promised.'

Veselý covered his eyes with his hand. There was a prolonged period of silence during which Klinger rejoiced that once again a bluff had paid off.

'It's true,' Veselý admitted at last, 'that I haven't yet managed to scrape together my part of the deal. But I will. This is my chance to make it big. Somehow I'll make it happen.'

'That's why you started clearing the site, isn't it? You couldn't make the deposit but you wanted to show the Russians that you were in earnest.'

Veselý nodded.

'And you couldn't complete the compulsory purchase of the cottages because you couldn't pay the compensation.'

'These are local people!' the deputy mayor cried. 'I could never leave them unpaid. I couldn't live with myself.'

Klinger collected together his papers and returned them to his briefcase.

Veselý was the very epitome of misery. 'What happens now?' he asked.

'I go back to Prague. It's probably best if we both forget this little chat for now. You haven't done anything illegal so far as I can see. But if you'll take my advice, you won't put any more in. I think it very likely that we'll be able to prove that the Russians have come by their money illegally and I'll get a proceeds of crime forfeiture warrant. Put them off as long as you can. Don't do any more work on the site. Who knows, perhaps in a few years people will be grateful that you spotted that your partners were crooks before they were all badly burned. But for the moment I'd like you to continue as usual. It's vital that the Russians don't discover I'm on to them. Do you understand?'

Veselý nodded.

'Of course, Mr Veselý, if I were to discover that you had said anything to them about our little chat I'd have to move in and confiscate everything. There would be arrests, publicity, humiliation. It wouldn't be very pleasant for you.'

'I understand,' said the deputy mayor, and the look on his face was ample testimony that he really did.


Lukas listened attentively to Slonský's account. 'I don't like it. One of the unwritten rules of policing is that we look after our own. If we can't prevent a death, we make sure we catch the man responsible. But it doesn't sound as if that ethos has reached Pardubice.'

'I wonder if Sedlák was ever a whistleblower? What made him so unpopular that his own colleagues aren't angry that he was killed?' Slonský asked.

They sat in silence for a few moments as each man thought through the possibilities, but neither could see why Sedlák's death might occasion indifference. It was Lukas who finally broke the silence.

'The runt of the litter.'

This gnomic pronouncement briefly caused Slonský to frown until he realised the point that Lukas was making.

'Of course! The one who needs the others most.'

'We need to look at the Pardubice criminal police to see who is most susceptible to pressure.'

'Doležal tells me that Klaberský is the newest lieutenant.'

'No more junior officers?'

'Two, but they have only been there a few months. I sense that this is a long story.'

'Well, I suspect that Klaberský is the one to target then. But you'd better do it. Life could get very difficult for Doležal if he tries. Unless you'd prefer me to go?'

'I'd much prefer that in the normal run of things, but you're leaving soon and we might need to put continuing pressure on him. I'd better go.'

'There may be a better option,' Lukas suggested.

'Really?' said Slonský hopefully.

'Major Rajka might be willing to do us a little favour. It is what he's paid for, after all. And this man Vondra won't dare to kick up a fuss if someone from the Office of Internal Inspection is nosing around his men.'

'Would Rajka do that?'

'Well, if there's any chance that the local chaps are impeding the investigation into the death of a police officer, of course he would. Let's see if he's around.'

Lukas consulted his internal telephone directory. The OII office was one of those telephone numbers that nobody would want to admit to remembering.

'He's on his way over.'

'Shouldn't we go to him? He outranks us, after all.'

Lukas allowed himself a slight smile. 'I imagine he likes to get out now and again. The atmosphere in OII is not jolly much of the time.'

'I'll go and fetch some coffees,' Slonský suggested.

'Good idea.'

Slonský just had time to collect three coffees — in proper cups, since a major was involved — and was climbing the stairs when he saw Rajka striding past. His was one of the more recognisable figures in the Prague headquarters, since he had been a keen wrestler in his younger days. Not quite one metre eighty tall, but with a chest and biceps that tested the tailor's art, Rajka would have earned top marks for deportment at any ladies' finishing school, having a straight spine and a well-balanced walk. It was notable that even people with blameless characters looked twitchy when they saw Rajka coming, and he liked it that way.

Rajka and Lukas were already speaking when Slonský entered and laid the tray on the desk.

'Congratulations on your promotion, Slonský,' said Rajka. 'And I wish you a happy retirement, Lukas.'

'Thank you. It will be a wrench leaving these fine people, but it's time. And my little health scare has concentrated my mind on having some time to myself before I pass on.'

Slonský still had nightmares about that "little health scare" when Lukas slumped to the floor of his office and Slonský had thought he was about to die in front of him. Luckily Dr Novák was there too, who was no use at all in treating a living patient but at least knew the telephone number for an ambulance.

'Now, explain to me about Pardubice,' commanded Rajka.

'The explosion on the evening of Liberation Day killed one of our officers, a Lieutenant Sedlák, who was a criminal policeman operating out of Pardubice but responsible largely for the area around Holice where he lived,' Slonský began.

'There were four casualties, weren't there?' Rajka interrupted.

'Yes, an engineer and a local man and his son also died. The pathologists believe that they were placed in a tight circle and a grenade was then dropped in the middle.'

'Ruthless.'

'Yes, Major. We're also aware, but have not publicized the fact, that a large self-propelled gun borrowed from the Czechoslovakian Army in 1968 was in the same field. Our assumption is that these men were killed because they stumbled across the gun.'

'I'm not going to go any further into your enquiry, Slonský. It'll only waste time and it's not my role. Explain to me why you have concerns about Pardubice.'

'Plainly with a lieutenant gone they were going to be short-staffed, so we deputed one of our lieutenants, Doležal, to go to Pardubice and give them a hand until they made a permanent appointment.'

'He's a good man,' Lukas chipped in. 'Over twenty years of experience with the police. Slonský, of course, retained overall control of the investigation.'

'But in your phone call you said that he was complaining of a lack of support.'

'Yes,' agreed Lukas, 'which is not like Doležal, who is normally very happy to work on his own. But I begin to suspect that it may be more than just a lack of support. Doležal reports indifference to the fate of a fellow officer.'

'I see. Well, we can't have that, can we? The makeup of the department is…?'

Lukas indicated that this was a question for Slonský.

'Vondra, Captain; three lieutenants, Staněk, Klaberský and poor Sedlák.'

'Presumably some juniors?'

'There are, but never seen. They seem to work directly for Vondra,' Slonský replied.

'An unusual arrangement and one that smacks of insecurity. I think I'll take a look.'

Rajka began to rise from his seat but was stopped by a further comment from Slonský.

'One small complication…'

'Out with it!'

'One of my officers is currently working undercover in Holice without the knowledge of the local detectives. I know it's highly irregular…'

'From what you tell me it's a damn good thing they don't know he's there. How is he contacting you?'

'He isn't. He's temporarily working with Poznar of the BIS.'

Rajka mulled this information over for a few moments. 'Poznar is a good man. It's best if that particular rock isn't turned over.'

Slonský breathed a quiet but heartfelt sigh of relief. There were people on OII who would have demanded Navrátil's recall and a full written explanation of this irregularity in triplicate, but fortunately Rajka was much more pragmatic.

'One more thing…' Slonský began.

'Yes?'

'Can I come?'

'You? Why?'

'If they tell you anything useful it would be good to be able to act immediately on it. Plus I want to see Vondra's smug backside getting a kicking.'

Rajka gave in. 'Some company on the drive might be nice. But you let me run things. If they suspect you're calling me in I'll be okay but they could make life very difficult for Doležal.'

'And me, I suppose,' said Slonský.

'Yes, but I don't care about you,' said Rajka. 'you're old enough to look after yourself.'

'Understood, sir,' Slonský responded. 'When do you want to go?'

'My car's round the back,' said Rajka. 'Get your coat. If it's important enough to do, it's important enough to do now.'

Slonský had never seen a car like Rajka's. It was brilliant white, glossy, well-kept, and the inside was immaculate, an adjective that had never been applied to any car that Slonský had driven. It had black leather seats that caressed his back and a dashboard full of switches, the purpose of many of which he could not begin to guess.

'What's this for?' he enquired.

'Heated seat.'

'And this one?'

'The other heated seat.'

'Right. And that?'

'Changes the waveband on the radio.'

Slonský had never been in a car that had more than one waveband before.

Rajka suddenly spoke loudly. 'Play country music.'

'I can't,' Slonský replied.

'I was talking to the car.'

Sure enough, after a couple of seconds the car was filled with the sound of a woman singing a dirge that Slonský could not quite understand but which appeared to express her regret at having chosen the wrong man.

'It can hear you?' he said.

'Voice responsive entertainment system,' Rajka answered.

'You mean a radio?'

'A voice responsive entertainment system is more than a radio,' Rajka protested. 'Hang on, we don't want to take all day. No point in having lights if you don't use them.'

He flicked a switch and blue lights began to flash from the radiator grille, encouraging cars in front of them to pull to one side and allowing Rajka to press harder on the accelerator. Slonský could not see exactly how fast they were going but the needle on the speedometer seemed to be a lot further round the dial than even he was used to.

Slonský sank back into the seat. Here he was, driving at very high speed in the company of a man who talked to cars.

Navrátil was almost regretting having gone to Pardubice now that everything had happened after he came back. He wanted to keep Poznar briefed but he had to be sure that he would not be overheard. The best way of doing that, he decided, was to use his mobile phone while he was out for a run, during which he would find some out of the way place from which to make the call.

This plan had soon hit an obstacle, which was that there were a lot of trees on either side of the track and the telephone signal found them uncongenial. It was not until he had run around two kilometres out of town and was approaching the village of Veliny that he dipped into a side lane and made his call.

Poznar came to the phone and listened attentively as Navrátil made his report.

'Good. That sounds very promising,' said Poznar. 'But don't get carried away. Keep your guard up and don't ask too many questions straightaway. Just let them think that you could be a useful recruit for them, and let them make the pace. Is everything else going all right?'

'Yes, thanks. Someone searched my room the other day.'

'Did they find the camera?'

'I don't think so.'

'Probably best if you don't take it with you for your first meeting. If they've got any suspicions, that might allay them.'

'Very good, sir.'

'I'll tell Slonský that you've been in touch and all is well.'

Poznar abruptly hung up, leaving Navrátil to consider briefly whether "well" was the word he would have chosen.


Slonský received the call from Poznar and relayed the message to Peiperová.

Rajka swept off the highway without, apparently, feeling any need to use a brake. Although Slonský had experienced some misgivings, he was bound to admit that Rajka could handle a car, though as they approached the police building he would have liked some earlier intimation that Rajka was going to come to a halt.

The major leapt from the car and glanced over his shoulder to check that Slonský had followed before using his remote control key to lock the doors. 'Daren't leave it open. Too much of an invitation to the local wide boys,' he explained. 'Nothing they like better than turning over a police vehicle.'

'But yours is unmarked.'

'They'll know. In any event, there's more fun in joy-riding one of those than a Trabant.'

Rajka flung the station door open and marched in, leaving Slonský to make his own arrangement. Rajka still had the lithe movement of the Olympic athlete he once was. His feet barely seemed to contact the ground before he moved on like a panther who had detected the scent of something edible.

The sergeant on the desk glanced up as Rajka approached but returned to completing some paperwork.

Rajka slid his identity card across the form. 'Good afternoon,' he said cheerfully. 'I have business here.'

'Do you have an appointment, sir?' asked the sergeant. Even Slonský, who was not normally sensitive to vibrations in the air, could tell that this was a mistake.

'We don't make appointments, sergeant,' Rajka responded. 'We come and go as we see fit. Now, if you'll just direct me to the regional crime team, I won't need to disturb your day any further.'

'Through the doors and up the staircase, sir. You'll find them to the right at the top of the stairs. Their names are on their doors.'

'Thank you, sergeant. Don't tell them we're on our way up. We'd like it to be a surprise for them.'

Rajka bounded up the stairs two at a time, leaving Slonský heartily glad that he was not an OII officer. He would be exhausted by ten o'clock every morning if this was their normal pace.

The sergeant had not been strictly accurate, because the door to the large office displayed the names of Staněk, Klaberský and Sedlák. Rajka pushed it open and walked in, holding his ID aloft.

'Office of Internal Inspection,' he announced. 'This is an official visit. And you are?'

'Klaberský, Lieutenant,' said the man at the desk to the right.

'Doležal, Lieutenant,' added a thin man at the desk to the rear left. A small office occupied the rear right, from which a rotund man emerged.

'What's going on here, then?' Vondra demanded.

'No, that's my line,' Rajka told him. 'OII, here on official business.'

'I haven't been informed…' Vondra began.

'No, and that's the way it's going to be,' Rajka completed the sentence for him. 'There are matters of concern and I will be speaking to each of you in turn. Those to whom I have not spoken will not speak to each other or that will be considered to be potentially interfering with my enquiries and may in itself lead to disciplinary action. You have the right to remain silent but a failure to answer a question may lead to adverse inferences being drawn. Do you all understand?'

Three voices offered a lacklustre assent.

'Note that agreement, Slonský. Now, as I understand things, you, Doležal, are a new arrival and therefore cannot know anything about the incidents that form the substance of my enquiry. You are therefore welcome to make yourself scarce.'

Whatever business Doležal had been conducting, he knew enough about the ways of the OII to need no second invitation to leave the room, and, indeed, the building.

Rajka pointed at the vacant chair to his immediate left. 'This officer — where is he?'

'Staněk is investigating a burglary, sir,' Klaberský explained.

'Good. If he comes back, tell him to wait for us. Don't contact him without my knowledge. Clear?'

176

Slonský was impressed. Rajka's whirlwind approach had knocked the wind out of the policemen's sails. He liked to think that he could put people off guard during questioning, but he was learning from Rajka, and he liked what he saw. There had been suggestions that Rajka had received his promotion based on his athletic prowess, but Slonský could see that he was good at his job. Not to mention being around eighty-five kilos of solid muscle and gifted with a disturbing willingness to smile as he made a man's life miserable.

'Now, Captain, it's only right to begin with the head of the department. Shall we use your office? Slonský, would you mind staying here and keeping an eye on Lieutenant Klaberský?'

Slonský had hoped to be invited into the sanctum, but then he reflected that he had been warned that he was only there under sufferance in the first place, and therefore meekly complied.

Rajka and Vondra withdrew, leaving Slonský sitting opposite Klaberský, who seemed rather uncomfortable.

'What's all this about?' he asked.

'I can't tell you,' Slonský answered.

'If there's been some sort of … misunderstanding, perhaps I can clear it up without all this fuss.'

'I doubt you can.'

'I haven't done anything.'

'No,' agreed Slonský, 'you haven't done anything. And among the things you haven't done is help to find the person who killed your colleague. Wouldn't you agree that's rather curious?'

'That's your job!' Klaberský objected. 'Are you blaming me for your failure?'

Slonský chuckled. 'You could say that. On the other hand…' Slonský lunged forward and grasped Klaberský at the throat.

The younger man was caught off balance and found his feet flailing as his chair was tipped back. The back of his head hit the wall before the top of the chair came to rest there, his feet waving helplessly in the air. 'It's as well for you that Major Rajka wants to talk to you later,' hissed Slonský, 'which prevents you and I having the discussion that I would like to have. But if he finds that anyone here has been less than diligent in finding the killers of a fellow police officer I shall be asking him if I can put some supplementary questions while he goes for a walk round town. Do I make myself clear?'

'I can't breathe!'

'If only that were true, but you must be breathing because I can hear you whimpering. Now, why aren't you giving Lieutenant Doležal the kind of support that he is entitled to expect?'

Slonský released his grip and allowed the front legs of Klaberský's chair to return to the floor.

'I've got nothing to say,' stammered Klaberský.

'Suit yourself,' Slonský told him. 'Just remember I'm only a big thug but Major Rajka is a very strong man with an Olympian grip and a terrible dislike of bent coppers. If you've got anything to say you'll get a more sympathetic hearing from me than you will from him.'

'You didn't sound very sympathetic a minute ago.'

'I'm not; but I'm a teeny bit more sympathetic than Rajka. He'll want you humiliated and thrown out of the police, whereas I'll be satisfied if you just die in office.'

'You can't say things like that to me!'

'I just did. Do you want me to write it down in case you forget it?'

The door opened and Rajka stepped out, closely followed by Captain Vondra, whose face was ashen.

'I think I'd like to talk to you now, Klaberský,' said Rajka.

Klaberský rose from his chair and edged round his desk. However he did it, he would have to go within a metre of Slonský, who took the opportunity to grab his arm as he walked past.

'Mind how you go,' Slonský said.

Rajka preceded Klaberský out of the small office and demanded the address of the building where Staněk was investigating the burglary. Vondra wrote it down, his first movement in nearly half an hour since Rajka had finished with him. Slonský had judged that his best way to keep the pressure on was not to speak to Vondra, so he had immersed himself in a copy of the police newspaper until Rajka indicated that it was time to move on.

'You will not speak to Staněk until I have done so,' Rajka ordered. 'Is that clear?'

There was a murmur of assent from Vondra and Klaberský.

'And you will not speak to each other about the discussions each of you has had with me. Remember that you are both under active investigation.'

Rajka swept from the room leaving Slonský to catch up, an effort that required a certain amount of jogging on Slonský's part before he could get close enough to talk.

'Won't they just compare notes now that we've left?' he asked.

'Of course they will.'

'And what exactly is "active investigation"?'

'It means I haven't got bored and shelved it. More to the point, if they've got any sense they'll stop doing whatever it is they're doing that I might be looking into.'

'Don't you have to tell them what you're investigating?'

'Strangely enough, no. At least, not at this stage. In about a fortnight I'll have to write to them telling them what the issues are, but let them sweat till then. By the way, I don't know what you said to Klaberský but he was nicely softened up. I don't often make officers of his experience cry.'

'I just suggested that he could be doing more to help us find who killed Sedlák.'

'That's good. I told him the same thing.'

They climbed into the car and Rajka reversed out of the parking place with no obvious checking of mirrors.

'Forgive my asking,' Slonský said, 'but why was Captain Lukas so confident that you would be prepared to get involved in this?'

'Because I'd do anything for him if I could. It goes back to when I was picked for the Olympic trials. I'd already used my leave allocation. Before the Wall came down I'd have been given as much time off as I needed, but these arrangements were frowned on after the end of Communism. Amateur sportsmen had to be genuine amateurs, so I switched shifts and took time off to enter competitions. He was in charge of my local station and I went to see him to say that I wanted to leave the police. He asked why, and I explained I couldn't let my big chance go. With no leave left to take, I'd have to resign to enter the trials. So he said he would do my shifts for me. I don't know any other officer who would have done that. For about six weekends over training camps he stood in for me, and then I got selected and had a week-long camp before we left. Somehow he managed to get me the time I needed. He even persuaded the other fellows in my section to do one extra unpaid shift each so that I could have my tilt at a medal. Then, of course, I went to the Olympics and came back without one.

Still, I had my chance, and I have Lukas to thank for it. He's a good man. He'll be missed.'

'Yes, he will,' replied Slonský, thinking — for the first time — what a hard act Lukas would be to follow.

Staněk did not seem to have been informed of their intentions, nor was he excited to see them. He listened to Rajka's questions, answered them tersely, but, so far as Slonský could tell, honestly, and then returned to his investigation.

'What do you think?' Slonský asked.

'Whatever is going on, I think he's not part of it, but he knows enough to know he doesn't want to be part of it. If he doesn't know what's going on it's because he has chosen not to know.'

'He seems to be a bit of a loner.'

'Not a bad thing to be if something untoward is happening.'

'Are we any further forward?' Slonský asked.

'I think so. I can't prove it, but I think there's something going on outside the police that Vondra and Klaberský know about but Staněk doesn't. They don't trust him to keep the secret so they haven't let him in on it. Any idea what it is?'

'We're suspicious about a plan to build a huge shopping mall near Holice.'

'Near Holice? Why the hell would they want a shopping mall at Holice?'

'I don't think the public there does. But somebody does. I think Sedlák stumbled across some evidence and was killed to keep him quiet. The others were murdered because they happened to be there at the time.'

Rajka unlocked the car for the journey back to Prague. 'I can follow that hypothesis. But if you're right, why is Klaberský in on it whereas Sedlák wasn't? I mean, Holice was in Sedlák's area but not in Klaberský's.'

*Damn,* thought Slonský. *No wonder he's already a major and I'm just about to make it to captain.*

# Chapter 13

Navrátil felt naked. It went against the grain to wear a jacket without a tie, but he thought it would make him look more revolutionary to have an open collar. You can't go around trying to wreck the system in a collar and tie.

Nerad was walking towards him, sunglasses perched on the top of his head and a broad smile on his face.

'Got your thesis? Good. They won't want you to read it but there may be some questions on your work.'

'Will there be many there?' asked Navrátil. That seemed a safe question.

'You never know. Usually we get fifteen to twenty, but on a good day we can double that. I didn't have long to tell people you were joining us, but I'll be disappointed if there aren't twenty there.'

He had no reason for disappointment. Navrátil counted twenty-four people in the room and another couple slinked in after the meeting had started. They were predominantly of Nerad's age, but there were a number of older men. He had seen a few when he had been collecting his questionnaires, and he recognised the only woman in the group as the person who had given him directions on his arrival in town.

Nerad called the meeting to order and explained that the discussion they had planned for their regular monthly meeting was being postponed because by great good fortune a scholar from Prague was in their midst with some stimulating ideas that he, Nerad, believed would find some resonance with them all. He introduced Michal Ondráček to them and invited Navrátil to explain what he had been doing in Holice.

Navrátil realised that a postgraduate student was likely to be fairly confident at presenting his findings and did his best to look as if speaking to meetings and conferences was something he had done plenty of times before.

He walked round in front of the table to make it clear that he knew his stuff so well he did not need notes. 'I am a postgraduate student at Charles University studying for a doctorate,' he began. 'My thesis looks at the degree to which Czech identity is lost when our country joins international organisations such as the European Union, and how we might preserve it. I will emphasise right at the start that this is not a question of whether we should be members of such bodies; I have my opinion, and you will have yours, but that is a different argument. My interest is in what happens when we decide to join, as we have done in the case of the EU.'

To his surprise, the audience was very attentive. He could see several heads nodding, and not because their owners were falling asleep.

'I may as well say that the first draft of my thesis expressed concern that our unique Czech heritage was being diluted. In my opinion, the rush to be accepted by the western world and to separate ourselves from Soviet domination has had a price, maybe a price not worth paying. You may disagree.'

There were several cries of "No!"

'Unfortunately for me my supervisor, Professor Jakub Hofmann, disagreed profoundly with my assessment. He acknowledges that this is a matter of opinion and that it is possible therefore that his view and mine will not coincide, but he argued that I had not done sufficient fieldwork asking ordinary Czechs what they thought. If we want to know what is in the hearts of Czechs we must go to the heart of the country, and Holice is right in the middle, roughly equidistant between Karlovy Vary in the west and Ostrava in the east.'

'We don't want the Euro!' someone called out, to general approbation.

'Now that makes my point,' claimed Navrátil. He was not sure whether it did or did not, but it was a debating trick he had often seen used by politicians. 'There is a headlong rush towards joining the Eurozone at the earliest possible moment, but have ordinary Czech people been asked for their views?'

There was a loud chorus of "No!"

'Our best young people, our future, are leaking away from this country. Friends, you can't get a good young plumber in Prague now! They're all living in London or Berlin.'

Navrátil had no evidence for this assertion, but he had heard it said in the police canteen and thought it would play well with this audience. He was right. He glanced at Nerad whose smile illustrated his delight at the way things were going.

'It is clear from the questionnaires that I have collected here in Holice that the majority of citizens share my misgivings. I consider this strong evidence that my original thesis is defensible and I intend to tell Professor Hofmann so. Certainly, there are other weaknesses that I will have to address; but I believe that I can demonstrate that there is a substantial section of the Czech public who want to remain defiantly Czech.'

'A majority!' shouted someone.

'Well, we mustn't overstate our case just yet,' counselled Navrátil. 'We can show a substantial minority, and I have no doubt that if our arguments are given a fair airing, the numbers who think like we do will increase.'

Whatever else he was planning to say was lost as his audience erupted in applause, some rising to their feet. Nerad shook his hand and smacked him enthusiastically on his back.

'Well done!' Nerad cried, and allowed the applause to continue unabated until its natural conclusion before raising both hands, unnecessarily, to beg silence before he summed up.

'What we always believed is confirmed. We are the authentic voice of the Czech people,' he claimed. 'Our Home is the standard bearer for our legitimate national aspirations. Who knows,' he added with that smug smile Navrátil was getting to know so well, 'maybe one day our soon-to-be Dr Ondráček will return to Holice to represent us in the Chamber of Deputies!'

Navrátil the police officer had become Ondráček the demagogue.

Navrátil had decided that the best way to get information out of Nerad was to pretend that he really did not want it, so when they met up on Sunday afternoon — Navrátil having declined to meet on Sunday morning because he wanted to go to Mass — Nerad was suitably oblique.

'I can understand that people would be drawn to our arguments,' Navrátil explained. 'After all, they're self-evidently right. But how are we going to convince over half the voters in this country to support us?'

'We don't need half,' explained Nerad. 'When did this country have anything other than a coalition government anyway? All we need is a big enough voice not to be ignored.'

There was some truth in this. The 2006 Elections had been so finely balanced that even very small parties were courted to try to get to the magic 50% plus one. If Nerad's group held a reasonable number of seats — and in the list system used in the Czech Republic that was never impossible — they would become serious players very quickly if they had as little as ten to fifteen per cent of the vote.

'Can we get to that?' Navrátil asked, trying to sound enthusiastic about the prospect of an ultra-nationalist party doing well.

'I think if we have people of your calibre, of course we can,' Nerad replied. 'You know as well as I do that if the average Czech sees Dr in front of someone's name they seem to think they must know everything about everything. Believe me, if we could get ten or twelve academics to stand for parliament I could see them getting elected. But we can't depend entirely on political debate. We need action too.'

'You mean demonstrations?'

'Of a sort,' said Nerad, smiling that crooked half-smile of his again.


Slonský had been for a walk.

'You did what?' asked Valentin. 'Where to?'

'Nowhere. I just looked out and thought it was a lovely morning, so I went for a walk. Not far, just through the park, listening to the birds coughing their little lungs up in the Prague air.'

'It's cleaner than it used to be. Remember when the steam trains used to puff back and forth?'

'It's a very nice city,' Slonský insisted. 'It's my home. I wouldn't want to be anywhere else.'

'Neither would I,' said Valentin, 'but I don't feel the need to walk round it to prove the point. I can admire the idea of Prague without actually putting myself to the trouble of experiencing it.'

'Do you know,' said Slonský, taking a long pull from his beer before continuing, 'I was looking at all these couples of my age strolling around and thought that could be me and Věra.'

Valentin spluttered, sending a spray of beer across the floor. 'Don't tell me you're becoming domesticated.'

'No, of course not. We're apart and we're staying apart. I'm just saying that once in a while it would be fun to spend a Sunday afternoon with her.'

'Fun? You're fifty-nine. You're not supposed to be having fun. Fun is for young people.'

'She wounded me, there's no denying it. She left me and I can't forget that. But she's been doing the odd little job around the flat and cooking me the occasional meal and it's been quite pleasant.'

'Give me a couple of thousand crowns and I can go and get you a woman who'll do all sorts of things for you that are more than "quite pleasant" and she won't expect you to take her for a walk on Sundays.'

'Don't be vulgar. This is jealousy speaking. Maybe you would like a woman to look after you too.'

'I had one. I called her Mother. She died, and I didn't replace her.'

'Věra is not a replacement mother.'

'If you say so.'

'I do. Nor would it mean that I would neglect my old and loyal friends. You could come with us.'

'I am not playing gooseberry to you two! I'd feel like a spare part or some kind of weird chaperone.'

'Don't worry, I haven't got the inclination for that kind of thing at my age.'

'Thank heavens for small mercies.'

'I just think it would be nice to have a bit of company when I retire.'

'You have. You've got me. And you said yourself you weren't planning to retire for as long as you could persuade the police force to keep you on.'

'I'm not. But you have to think ahead. It would look pretty transparent if I suddenly started spending time with her three years from now, wouldn't it?'

'So what you really mean is that it would be nice to go for a walk with her three years from now?'

'Of course. What did you think I meant?'

Navrátil was curious. He had decided that he should write up the results of his questionnaires because that was what a real student would do, so he spent Monday morning in his room and only ventured out to the café to get some lunch. Nerad was already sitting there.

'I thought you'd turn up here sooner or later,' he said.

'Sorry, if I'd known you wanted me I'd have come out sooner. I was just writing up my work.'

'Of course. And it's given me the chance to catch up with Aunt Liliana.'

'Aunt Liliana?'

'The café owner. She's not my real aunt. She's my mother's cousin's daughter or something of the sort.'

'She's been very helpful to me,' said Navrátil.

'She's a good sort. Very sympathetic to our cause too.'

'Perhaps you can explain something to me,' Navrátil said, lowering his voice. 'When I was first here, she warned me to be careful of a man who she said was a policeman. Why would she do that?'

'A local man?'

'No, I think this one had been sent to replace the one who was killed.'

'Oh, old Sedlák. Aunt Liliana draws a distinction between our local police and the ones from the regional HQ in Pardubice. She's grown up with the local police. We know them and they know us. Nothing much happens here and they don't need to get too heavy with us. The Pardubice mob aren't as accommodating, that's all.'

'But the locals must be busy after that explosion?'

'That won't be local men,' said Nerad. 'If it were they would already have arrested them. It was probably some group of gipsies who shouldn't have been there, I wouldn't be surprised. But in any event the Pardubice police will be dealing with it. She was probably warning you that they'll try to pin it on anybody who doesn't fit in, or doesn't have an alibi.'

'Well, I'm grateful for the tip-off,' said Navrátil. 'It isn't always easy proving your innocence.'

'If they try to pin anything of that sort on you,' said Nerad, 'you get in touch with me. My family isn't without influence. I'll get my uncle to pull a few strings.'

'Thanks,' stammered Navrátil. 'That's good to know.'

'We've got to cover each other's backs in this world,' said Nerad. 'Fancy a walk? I want to talk to you about something and we can't do it here.'

Nerad looked around the park to ensure that nobody was within hearing range.

'You'll know, of course,' said Nerad, 'that the American President is coming here next month.'

'Yes, I think I read that somewhere,' said Navrátil.

'There'll be a lot of press coverage. The ideal time for us to make a statement, wouldn't you say?'

'I suppose so. So are you planning to disrupt his visit?'

'We certainly are. In a way that the world cannot ignore. This government will be shown up as the bunch of incompetents they are.'

'What are you — we — going to do?'

'It's still in the planning stage,' said Nerad. 'I just wanted to check that you agreed in principle because you'll be playing a major part in our action. Assuming you agree, of course.'

'It's a little hard to say whether I agree when I don't know what you're planning.'

'Don't worry, we're not going to ask you to kill the President! Your role is smaller but vital. You know your way around Prague, and we don't. We need someone to plot out our routes to avoid the areas where the police will be concentrating.'

The awkwardness — not to mention the irony — of Navrátil's position was not lost on him. The terrorists wanted him, an undercover police officer, to help them evade the police. It occurred to him that if they were going to be caught red-handed with all the evidence that Poznar would want, he was going to have to get them past the security cordon.

'Of course,' he said.


'Why are you wearing uniform?' Slonský asked.

'Because you'd arrest me if I wasn't,' Mucha replied.

'I meant why not civvies?'

'I'm working. Remember I told my wife I was helping you out on an enquiry today, which meant that unfortunately I wouldn't be able to carry the shopping for her and her sister. And that happens to be true, since we're on police business.'

'But you're on loan to the detective branch today, so you don't have to wear uniform.'

'No,' conceded Mucha, 'but you remember the time we raided that warehouse together?'

'The one where I ended up with a stray bullet in my backside?'

'That's the one. Well, if any clothes are going to get ruined they're going to be police issue, not my own.'

'Nobody is going to shoot at us. I just want to look at the crime site with a fresh pair of eyes and maybe question one or two people in Holice.'

Slonský dropped the car into third gear. Since they had been in fifth before, this caused Mucha to jerk forward.

'What was that all about?'

'Almost missed the turn there. That's because you're distracting me with chatter. Did the coffee spill over?'

'No, you're fine.'

Slonský patted the car's built-in cup holders with affection. 'Best idea ever. It takes a Czech to come up with something like that.'

They parked opposite the entrance to Miss Valachová's field, Slonský pulling up with two wheels on the grass bank so that Mucha stepped straight into a muddy puddle.

'So this is where it all happened?'

'Yes. Come through the gate and I'll show you.'

Slonský indicated the crater left by the grenade, the indentations left by the self-propelled gun still visible in the earth, and the approximate point where blood-stained shards of metal had been found that were not linked to the four victims. To his surprise Mucha immediately left the field without a word.

Thinking that his old friend had been overcome by it all, Slonský hurried after him, only to find Mucha pacing along the far verge, occasionally bouncing on the balls of his feet to look over the hedge into the field,

'Are you all right?' asked Slonský.

'It's all nonsense, isn't it?' replied Mucha.

'Is it? What is?'

'This idea about the gun in the field.'

'What's nonsensical about it? You can see it was there.'

'I'm not disputing that. It's how long it was there.'

'It must have been there overnight because of the rain not having reached the ground between the tracks.'

'Yes, but basically a self-propelled gun is the bottom half of a tank, right? In this case, a T34. But it's not just a two-dimensional smudge on the grass. It has height too. And there's no way that anyone walking along the grass opposite couldn't have seen it. Let's assume that they've covered it with a tarpaulin or something similar. It's still a big hump sticking up where no hump should be. If it didn't attract Sedlák's attention on the way out, why should it do so on the way back?'

Slonský took his hat off so he could scratch his head. It helped him think, he thought. 'Maybe he was chatting?'

'Maybe. Of course, with no pavement he should be walking facing the traffic, so he'd actually have a better view going out than coming back.'

'Okay, I've got the point. So what are we supposed to make of this?' Slonský asked.

'Let's assume that with a cover over it the gun looked like something else — some kind of tractor, for example. So it doesn't get noticed. But when they come back, it doesn't have a cover on, because it's about to be moved.'

'Well, we know it was moved straightaway. It was moved and then the witnesses were killed. It has to be that way because the grenade fragments weren't hammered into the soil by the weight of the gun passing over them.'

'These things don't just start first time and drive off, Josef. They'd have checks to do. I think if Sedlák investigated it's because he saw or heard it moving.'

Slonský was feeling a little disgruntled that he had not noticed this himself, but conceded the logic involved. 'So if the explosion was heard a little after six o'clock, maybe the gun was planned to be moved at six?'

'You'd need a crew to get it ready, open gates and so on. And moving it at the end of Liberation Day when there may be other military vehicles on the go would make a good plan.'

'So why didn't they wait until there was nobody about?'

'You've got somebody with little experience trying to drive a tank through a gateway without ripping the hedge up and betraying the secret. And they parked it at an awkward angle to get it out, parallel to the hedge. He'd have to drive up the field a bit to get the right angle, so he's going to be going slowly. There probably wasn't anyone around when they started, but by the time he'd manoeuvred it to get out the metal detectors had turned up and seen what was going on. And, I'd reckon, they recognised the people moving the gun, otherwise they could just have been tied up.'

'I don't think that follows. Maybe they were killed because they spotted the gun, not because they knew the people.'

'Maybe. But would it really matter? We're looking for the gun now anyway, so killing them hasn't made a difference to that.'

'The trouble with you, Mucha,' opined Slonský, 'is that you're thinking rationally, whereas most terrorists don't. At least not in line with any kind of reason that the rest of us can follow.'

'They can't know the metal detectors will turn up, so it can't be premeditated. It's impulsive. There was some good reason why they needed to kill. Merely having the gun doesn't do it — they could tie them up and leave one man to guard them with a pistol while they spirited the gun away.'

'Maybe they didn't have time. If the plan was to move the gun at six o'clock maybe someone else would be waiting for them at six or shortly afterwards. Somebody has to ensure that the receiving site is ready for them, after all. One badly parked car could scotch their entire plan. And you know how good we Czechs are at badly parking cars.'

'A T34 chassis isn't going to be held up by a parked car, Josef. It can roll over it and reduce it to a large sardine tin.'

Slonský gave his rear end a thoughtful scratch. 'They'd kept this secret for the best part of forty years, I suppose. They're not going to recklessly give it away one Tuesday afternoon. It's much more likely that they always planned to keep their secret and that everything they're doing is geared towards achieving that.'

'Exactly the point I'm making,' said Mucha.

'Yes, but I'm making it better,' said Slonský.

'That's a matter of opinion.'

'So we're back to the key question: why move it at all? They move it on Liberation Day, when it may just attract less attention than any other day. They do it in the late afternoon when people are going home or indoors eating. Fine — but those are mitigating the risk. They could avoid the risk if they don't move it at all. So what made them do that?'

'Are they planning to use it soon?'

'That's my fear.'

'Well, the obvious time to have a show of force is just before an election. But there are none scheduled for this year. There are a lot next year, beginning with the presidential election. But that wouldn't explain why you'd move now.'

'President Bush is coming.'

Mucha, a man who was normally regarded as utterly unflappable, stood wide-eyed. 'Next month, isn't it?'

'He arrives on June 4th.'

'That's it! You don't need an army or a mass uprising. If Bush wants NATO to station arms here, what better way to scupper that deal than by showing that nationalists might steal them?'

'That doesn't give us very long to get to the bottom of this. It's less than a fortnight away. I'd better give Poznar a call.'

To Slonský's surprise, Poznar did not seem too concerned.

'That possibility had crossed our minds,' he remarked. 'But we're already taking serious security precautions to protect the President.'

'You think they might use the gun to attack the President?'

'They won't get close. If they hit his cavalcade from a distance it would have to be a very lucky shot.'

'Permit me to observe,' Slonský commented, 'that a shell from a 105mm gun landing on a Presidential car is likely to do more than scratch the paintwork. And I know your men are trained to throw themselves in front of an assassin's bullet but that isn't going to work too well here.'

'Granted,' Poznar agreed, 'but anything short of a direct hit won't pierce the armoured steel.'

'Why do it when he's in the car? We know to the centimetre where he'll be standing during the playing of the national anthems when he meets our President.'

'Why not leave these matters to those who spend their lives worrying about them, Slonský? Of course I've already told them there's a self-propelled gun unaccounted for. They were concerned to hear that.'

'I bet they were. I'd be even more concerned if they weren't.'

'I also told them the best detective in the Czech Republic was looking for it.'

'Oh, wonderful! Now it'll be my fault if that lucky shot takes the American President out.'

'You'll be pleased to hear that they have such faith in your ability that they downgraded the risk score.'

'That's nice.'

'By half a point.'

'Amateurs.'

# Chapter 14

Navrátil eased open the door of the conference room and peeked in. A familiar figure was perched on a stepladder and although her back was towards him this did not hinder Navrátil's recognition of her.

Peiperová descended gracefully, looked about her and kissed him as energetically as the fact that they were in a room with two unguarded entrances would permit.

'It's good to see you,' she said.

'Not as good as it is to see you. And to be Jan Navrátil again. I've come to the conclusion that I don't really like Michal Ondráček.'

'I've never liked him,' Peiperová confessed. 'He keeps me from you. Is that your uniform?'

Navrátil was holding a garment cover over one arm.

'Yes. I've given it a quick press but it hasn't been out of its cover for over a year. I just hope the moths haven't been chewing it.'

'It'll be strange seeing you in uniform. I've never seen you or Lieutenant Slonský in full dress.'

'It'll be Captain Slonský in a few hours.'

'It already is, officially. He's got the letter, and his insignia have been attached to his new uniform.'

'He's got a new one, just for this?'

'He needed a new one. The old one didn't fit too well.'

'Have you started the new job yet?'

'As good as. Technically, I start on June 1st, but I've spent so much time in the new office learning the ropes and doing induction training that I've been there almost every day for the last fortnight. How are you getting on in Holice?'

'Fine. I think I'm making some headway. But let's not talk shop now. We've got a party ahead of us.'

'Good point. Make yourself useful and hold this banner while I pin the other end.'

'We've only got one stepladder,' Navrátil objected.

'I know. But there are tables and you're always telling me you're light on your feet.'


Slonský turned sideways to admire the cut of his uniform once again. It was a long time since he had worn clothes that fitted properly. Dipping one shoulder to admire the epaulette again he donned his cap and practised a salute.

'You look very smart,' said Věra.

'Do you think so?'

'I wouldn't have said it otherwise. Come here while I brush the back of the collar.'

Slonský obeyed without protest.

'Do you think you can keep your hands out of your pockets?' Věra asked.

'Of course.'

'I meant right now.'

'Oh.'

'And this evening too. The uniform looks sharper if your arms are hanging loosely.'

'You make me sound like an orangutan. What are you going to wear?'

'That's easy. I've only got one presentable outfit.' Věra opened the wardrobe door and produced it.

'How long have we got till we need to be there?' asked Slonský.

'Around three hours. Why? Are you nervous?'

'Me? No. I just wondered if we've got time for a little shopping.'

Věra looked radiantly happy. She had been worried that her presence might be awkward, given that presumably Slonský would have attended social events without her for the last thirty years or so, but Slonský had forestalled any embarrassment by giving police social events a wide berth all this time; as, indeed, he would have preferred to do with this one were he not expected to turn up to receive his promotion.

Lukas in particular had made her welcome. As soon as they arrived he introduced her to his wife and daughters, which enabled him to slip off for a quick word with Slonský.

'I can't remember how long it is since I saw Věra. She's looking well.'

'She's aged a bit.'

'Haven't we all? And since it's been a generation or so, she's entitled.'

'I suppose.'

'My wife was so looking forward to meeting her. They seem to be getting along famously.'

'They've got something in common, I guess. They can chat about the difficulties of having a policeman for a husband.'

'Not for much longer.' Lukas downed the last of his fruit juice. 'It's all right for you, Josef. You don't have to give a speech.' He pointed to Slonský's glass. It looked as if contained water, but Lukas' nose had detected that it was largely schnapps.

'You should have one of these, sir. It might loosen your inhibitions when the time comes.'

'I'm quite content for my inhibitions to remain tight, thank you. This is trying enough as it is. I'd much have preferred to sneak out of the back door and just go home.'

'Then you would deprive Peiperová of her big moment, sir. She tells me the collection went awfully well.'

'Did it? How gratifying. Not because I want a big present, Heaven forbid, but it's good to know that my efforts here have not been entirely unappreciated. Any idea what I'm getting?'

'No, sir, but I can tell you this much. It needed two sheets of wrapping paper.'

'Two sheets? My word.'

The Director had arranged with Slonský that when he headed to one end of the room at ten minutes past the hour, Slonský would make for the opposite wall. The idea was that he would then walk the length of the room, maximising the opportunity for applause and making it much less likely that anyone would fail to pay attention. This was reinforced by Peiperová's energetic clearance of the centre to make a broad corridor down the middle for the conquering hero to process. When the Director cleared his throat and began to speak, Slonský was in position and had time to look around.

He had never seen Navrátil in uniform before. The door at the far end opened and Doležal slipped in, also in uniform. Doležal carefully edged his way in and found a place beside Navrátil, tapping his younger colleague on the shoulder and murmuring a greeting as he did so.

Dvorník looked a complete mess. Slonský appraised him ruthlessly as only a recent convert to tidiness could do. His uniform was rarely given an outing and had clearly been fitted some time ago or bought second hand from a much smaller man. The fact that only one button was done up was adequate evidence for the augmentation of Dvorník's physique, and since he had always tended towards the fuller figure anyway, the overall effect was of an overstuffed scarecrow.

The Director had concluded his introductory remarks and invited Captain Slonský to receive his new commission. Slonský resisted the temptation to march even when the audience broke into rhythmic clapping. He was sure he heard Věra shouting "Bravo!" and Mucha broke off applauding to wish Slonský good luck by shaking both fists. The envelope was passed with a smooth movement and a handshake which was held while the photographer captured the moment. Any thought that Slonský might have had of addressing his adoring following was efficiently dispelled by a gentle shove in the small of the back from the Director, so Slonský simply walked back to join Věra at the side of the room a little way from Navrátil.

The Director now invited Captain Lukas to step forward, a cue for Peiperová to duck behind a table and produce an oddly shaped parcel wrapped in blue and gold paper, which she placed on the table beside the Director. After a brief biography and an encomium on Lukas' integrity and character, the Director handed it over to the applause of all around. Urged to unwrap it, Lukas did so, to reveal a violin case. Knowing that a good detective takes nothing for granted he flipped the catches to check that there was a violin inside, which he removed and examined. It was beautiful, a chestnut colour with some black detailing, and it felt good under his chin.

'I haven't played since I was a boy,' he protested when they demanded a tune, and limited himself to a fairly rusty scale or two before adding, 'but I shall enjoy playing with my daughters who will teach me how to do it better.' He began his speech.

'I'm not one for public speaking, as many of you will know, but neither am I a man to shirk his duty, so here goes.'

After reviewing his career and praising the young police officers in whose career he had, perhaps, been privileged to play a small part, he turned to the future.

'Retirement has been made easier by the knowledge that I am to be succeeded by my old colleague and friend, now Captain, Josef Slonský. There may, of course, have been other equally deserving candidates,' he added diplomatically, 'but Captain Slonský and I have known each other for many years. He will know how many; I cannot say that I remember precisely. But I do recall the first case we tackled together.' He consulted his notes briefly. 'I was still a Lieutenant then, and we were in a car on the outskirts of Prague when we were asked to sort out a domestic disturbance. There was a woman who was a regular churchgoer. Her husband was not and chose to stay at home. What she did not know was that while she was at church services her husband and her neighbour were conducting an irregular liaison. When the neighbour heard the church bell toll she would wait a few minutes, then sneak next door. On this particular Sunday she did so, rushing in and embracing her lover, only to find that the wife had not yet left and was still in the bedroom. You can imagine that quite a scene ensued.'

Slonský chuckled as he recalled the events.

'I had never been required to separate two fighting women before. Indeed, I don't think I had ever seen such a thing, and I had no idea how to go about it. The normal techniques for sorting out fighting men seemed inappropriate somehow, and I was floundering until Slonský picked up the neighbour, flung her over his shoulder and returned her to her home. He then suggested that since no legal offence had been committed, we should leave those involved to hold such discussions as they thought necessary. And that, you see, is Slonský. Decisive, practical but also suspicious, because we sat outside in the street for half an hour in case we needed to intervene again. At least I did; Josef went to obtain some coffee and pastries to make the waiting more enjoyable.'

The audience sensed that they should applaud but Lukas raised a hand; he had not yet finished the story.

'But he is also thorough. He went to the church to find out why the bell had been rung early, and discovered that two cats had been having a fight in the belfry and had become entangled in the ropes.'

The evening was warm and clear, though the continued dry spell suggested that there might be lightning before long. Lukas held the door open for his wife and daughters, then ushered Věra through. She was unused to such courtesy but thanked him and continued her conversation with Mrs Lukasová as they descended the steps. Slonský brought up the rear.

'Well, old friend, thanks to the leave I have due I think that's the last time I shall walk through those doors.'

'I hope not,' said Slonský. 'We'll see you around for a long time to come.'

'If invited. But I always think it's a mistake to come back in other circumstances. People tolerate it at first but it's not healthy. I must make the break and settle into retired life.'

'You have your violin to practise,' said Slonský, helpfully pointing to it in case Lukas had forgotten what he was carrying.

'Yes! Yes, I have. But, you know, I have no idea how anyone knew that I had played it as a boy. I don't think I've ever said anything about it.'

Slonský could prove nothing, but the fact that Peiperová had telephone numbers for the two Lukasová girls seemed to him to suggest a possible line of enquiry.

Lukas extended his hand. 'Goodbye, Josef. And good luck. I hope you enjoy your time in charge as much as I have.'

Slonský took the proffered hand and grasped it firmly. He hoped the shadow cast by the peak of his cap was obscuring any glistening on his cheek. 'Goodbye, sir. Enjoy your retirement. You deserve it.'

'Thank you. But don't be a stranger. You know where I live.'

It crossed Lukas' mind for a moment that he had no idea where Slonský lived. Very few did; but it seemed like prying to ask.

'That's very kind, sir. I'll be sure to drop in.'

Impulsively Lukas embraced his former subordinate. 'You do that.'

# Chapter 15

Year one of the era of Slonský began with a few changes. He looked round Lukas' old office and decided he did not want to move from where he was. On the other hand to leave it vacant was to invite its reallocation to another team. His solution was to designate it as the workspace of Officers Navrátil and Peiperová.

'Does that mean I'll be working from here, sir?' asked Navrátil, who was slightly perturbed by this turn of events.

'Not at all. A keen-eyed lad like you will observe that there is only one desk.'

'Yes, sir.'

'That is Officer Peiperová's desk. When she returns, you can move in if you want, but for now this is hers. It would be good if you could spend an hour or two in here from time to time to make it look untidy. Well, type out your names on a card and stick it on the door, lad. That'll be a job well done, then we can stop for a coffee.'

They walked down the stairs to the canteen, Navrátil finding that he needed to move rather faster than he was used to in order to keep up.

Poznar listened carefully to Navrátil's report. 'Do you know what exactly they're planning to do?' he asked.

'I'm afraid not. I'm hoping they'll let me know if I continue to ingratiate myself with them.'

'If they want to get inside the cordon that doesn't sound like the use of a large artillery piece,' said Slonský. 'I imagine that's big enough to make its own way in.'

'But it doesn't need to get inside the barriers,' Poznar pointed out. 'It can fire a few shots from outside, no doubt. After all, it has an effective range of twelve to fourteen kilometres.'

'Fifteen kilometres,' Slonský said, 'according to Dr Kohoutek.'

'I'm not sure the extra kilometre makes much difference, Slonský.'

'It does if you're standing in it when the gun goes off.'

'Well, anyway, the question is what happens after the gun has been fired. Confusion and casualties, no doubt, but what are Nerad and Our Home planning to do in the immediate aftermath? Are they equipped to mount some sort of coup?'

'Hardly,' said Navrátil. 'There are only a couple of dozen of them and most of them are bar-room revolutionaries.'

'There may be other branches elsewhere,' Slonský commented.

'Yes, but they'll all be the same size. If they could rummage up five hundred men in the whole of the country I'd be surprised. The most they can hope for is some publicity stunt.'

'I think they've been working on some banners, sir,' said Navrátil. 'I haven't seen them personally, but there's something in a small industrial workshop Nerad came close to showing me at the weekend.'

'A small industrial workshop big enough to take a self-propelled gun?' asked Slonský.

'No, sir. The door is too small.'

Poznar tapped his pen on the table top while he was thinking. 'You'd best get back to Holice before they wonder where you've got to, Navrátil. Thanks for all you're doing. It's good work.'

'Thank you, sir.'

Slonský wrapped a long arm around Navrátil's back. 'There'll be a desk for you when you get back, lad. I'm not quite sure where it will be, but you'll still have a desk.'

Valentin glanced up when he detected a shadow falling across his glass. 'Hello, stranger,' he said.

'It hasn't been that long,' Slonský argued.

'It seems it. I was beginning to feel used and discarded.'

'Nonsense. You just want a scoop.'

'Of course I do. And in view of the material assistance I've given you I feel entitled.'

'Stop pouting. You'll get your scoop as soon as I know what's going on.'

'I thought you'd know by now. It's not like you not to wrap up a case that's been going for over a month.'

'Only just over a month. I have some pieces of the jigsaw. But when I try to put them together I get a really weird picture.'

'Such as?'

'There's a huge building development being built with Russian money. There's an antique 105mm pop-gun someone in the country. There's a right-wing nationalist group who may or may not have the gun but are planning something for the time of the visit of the American President. And there are a bunch of local police who appear not to be too bothered by any of this.'

'Are they involved in it?'

'It's the obvious inference but I'll leave that to Major Rajka to ferret out.'

'Rajka? Rajka who used to twist people's arms off for fun?'

'That's him. Nice chap.'

'Till you cross him.'

'No, we understand each other,' said Slonský. 'He's very straightforward. Keep on the straight and narrow and he's your mate. Get into anything dodgy and he'll reshape your backside with his toecap. We're on the same wavelength.'

'Pleased to hear it. So why are you loafing around in here instead of busting a gut to round up some criminals?'

'We've already got plenty. The jails are full. We've got to stop arresting them until some of the others have served their sentences and made a bit of space.'

'And the real reason?'

'I can't think of a way to force the case open. There's something that is staring me in the face, but I can't see it yet. I will though. I always do.'

Valentin was concerned. 'You don't think your powers are declining since you cut your beer consumption?'

'Do you think so?'

'The old Slonský had a brain like a purring locomotive.'

'That's true. And I do think better with a bit of lubrication oiling the cogs.'

'Tell you what. I'll break my five plus two routine and have one with you. Just to keep you company.'

'Good idea.'


The evening in Prague for Lukas' retirement had been very welcome to Doležal, so much so that he was contemplating spending the weekend there rather than hanging around Pardubice. Given that it was Friday, the prospect was growing ever more appealing.

He lifted his mug to discover that it was empty, so he walked to the staff room to replenish its contents. Somebody had been reading the new issue of the police newspaper and had left it on the small table that they all had to share.

Doležal rarely bothered with it, but his attention was attracted by a large photograph of the Director shaking hands with Captain Lukas as he presented him with the violin. It was a very good photograph.

Doležal had heard the expression that one's blood ran cold but he had never experienced it.

Until now.

He left his mug and ran to the car park, taking the paper with him. He had an urgent telephone call to make.

'Have you seen the police newspaper?' barked Doležal when Slonský returned to the office and answered his phone.

'Can't say I have,' replied Slonský.

'You need to ring Navrátil and get him out of there. His cover's blown. There's a photo of Captain Lukas' retirement and you can see him clearly in a police uniform. Somebody here has seen it, because it's been left open in the staff room. I tried ringing Navrátil but his phone isn't being answered.'

'I wondered why it was ringing. It's here in his drawer. We took it off him and gave him a new one. Have you removed the paper?'

'I found two copies and they're both in the boot of my car.'

'Good work. Leave it with me.'

Slonský rang Poznar and explained the situation.

'Jesus Maria, why did you let them take photos?' asked Poznar.

'I didn't actually arrange it,' Slonský protested. 'Ask the Director.'

'Stop waffling and get off the line,' Poznar growled. 'I've got to find Navrátil.'

Navrátil admired heroes but he had no wish to be one. As soon as Poznar rang to tell him to get out, he threw his clothes into his bag, collected his other belongings and left. His landlady was out so he had no opportunity to explain to her, but she had been paid anyway. Walking as quickly as he dared go without drawing attention to himself, Navrátil soon rounded the corner leading to the train station, and immediately doubled back. Nerad and one of his thugs were pacing the street in front of it, presumably having been tipped off. Nerad's expression demonstrated that he was very unhappy, and if he could get his hands on Navrátil the young policeman would be very unhappy too. There was no way that he could get to the train without being seen.

His next thought was the bus stop, but it was soon clear that Our Home had that covered too. A couple of the men who had been the most fervent cheerleaders when he spoke so recently were now prowling the bus stands, and Navrátil was fairly sure that the large wrenches they were carrying were not intended for use on the buses' wheels.

Navrátil ducked into an alleyway to think. There was a small railway halt to the north-east of the town that he had seen on his runs. It was perhaps five kilometres away, but if he could get there he could catch a train. It would have to be one going in the wrong direction because he could not risk coming back through the centre of town, but if he could get to Týniště nad Orlicí he could then catch a train running back to Prague by the northern route. However, zastavka Holice, the little train halt, lay along the road that passed the main train station, so he would have to run by a roundabout way, and he had jogged along those paths often enough to know that there was little cover and he would be clearly visible from some distance. He could not risk it. There had to be some other place where he would be safe.

He could think of only one option; and after a few moments an idea occurred as to how he might reach it. It would involve a particularly wicked sin, but he hoped God would understand.

Peiperová had been daydreaming at her new desk. In her mind's eye she replayed everything that she had learned about the murder of the four men at Holice and tried to visualise the events in sequence. It was then that she realised what had been troubling her.

The Director was out of his office at a meeting, so, acting on her own initiative, as she had been told so often a good policewoman does, she scribbled a note for him, taped it to his computer screen and ran along the corridor to find Slonský. She turned breathlessly into the room she still thought of as Lukas' office only to find it empty, though with her name on the door, which was a pleasant surprise. Running a few metres further she burst into Slonský's office to find him making short work of a ham roll.

'Okay, I'm busted,' he said, 'but if you were trying to catch me out you didn't have to put such effort into it.'

'It's not that, sir. I've just realised what has been troubling me about what we heard at Holice.'

Slonský nodded to the chair opposite him. 'Park yourself there, girl, and let's hear it.'

Peiperová stuttered as she rushed to get the words out.

'Take your time,' Slonský advised her. 'I've achieved damn all in four weeks, so a few more minutes isn't going to make a difference.'

'It's to do with what Jiří Jeníček said, sir.'

'Remind me again who Jiří Jeníček is.'

212

'The old man who looks after Miss Valachová's field, sir. He told me he heard the bang, then he went into the house to check his wife was safe, and then he walked up the road. I thought it took him a while to find his wife, but it's a very small house. It can't have taken more than a minute or two. Then he walks up the road to the field, and he says that took him about five minutes. But long before he got there, he saw Captain Forman's car parked in the middle of the road outside his house, and Forman himself was by the field. Now, Forman is no youngster and he's not built for speed. So how did he get to the site of the explosion so quickly?'

Slonský slapped his hand on the desk top. 'Of course! I was hung up on why nobody in the pub heard the bang, but if they didn't then Forman certainly can't have done, because the police station is quite a way further off. Oh, the little scamp lied to us!'

'It's worse than that, sir. Given the time it would take to drive from the police station to the field, I think Forman must have set off before the explosion.'

'And you must be right, young lady, because I think that too.' Slonský grabbed his coat and hat. 'Come along! We're going to get ourselves a nice fast car, ideally with those flashing lights and a siren, and because you've been good you can drive it to Holice with the whole lot going.'

Navrátil never claimed to be a saint, but he tried, so far as he was able, to live a blameless life. It therefore went against the grain for him to contemplate theft, but he salved his conscience by telling himself that he had no intention to deprive his victim permanently. It was more of a forced loan, really. Of course, the fact that he was burgling a church would ordinarily have started Confession with Father Anton on the wrong foot, but at least it wasn't Father Anton's church.

Since he had been in Holice he had attended Mass at the little church which, by happy chance, adjoined the bus stands but was screened by a few trees. Navrátil decided that the circumstances justified him in walking on the grass instead of keeping to the path as instructed, and he was able to slide in through the church door undetected.

St Martin's was a delicate lemon and white building, but wonderfully cool inside. Navrátil had seen the priest head for the vestry after the services so he knew where to go. He just hoped that the people of Holice were a trusting lot who had no love of keys.

The vestry proper was unlocked, probably because there were no valuables there. Navrátil opened the doors in turn until he found what he wanted, then removed a few items from his bag before stowing it in the cupboard. He found a pen and a scrap of paper and left a note for the priest in which he apologised for what he had done, explained that he would return when he could to retrieve his bag, and informed the priest that if he telephoned Captain Josef Slonský at the telephone number below all would be explained. At least, he hoped it would. He then had the audacity to ask for the priest's prayers to keep him safe.

Looking out cautiously, Navrátil emerged from the vestry with only the shoulder bag in which he kept his laptop, his clothes concealed by the black priestly cassock he had borrowed, and his face at least partly shielded by a clerical soup plate hat.

As he went out into the street the old flower-seller on the corner bowed her head respectfully. Navrátil thought he ought to bless her or something of the sort, but made do with a cheery "Good morning!" before setting off on his long walk.

Doležal was trying to complete a report on a burglary when his concentration was disturbed by something being thrown in front of him. It was a copy of the police newspaper.

'You knew,' Klaberský snarled. 'You knew there was an undercover cop working here and you didn't tell us.'

A poll of police in the Prague headquarters might well have led one to suppose that Doležal came a close second to Klinger in a list of officers least likely to be useful when rough stuff starts, but when Klaberský launched his right fist in Doležal's direction he was hampered by having to punch across a desk, which gave Doležal just enough time to grab the wrist and pull. As usual, Klaberský reacted by trying to draw his wrist back, taking the power out of the punch, and Doležal yanked Klaberský's arm outward and as far backward as he could manage across the desk. Klaberský gripped his shoulder in pain, giving Doležal the opening he needed to get out of the room. He had no idea where he was going, but his journey would begin by looking for the nearest exit.

Slonský had decided that he ought to keep Major Rajka informed but he did not want to make an enforced detour to the OII offices before going to Holice. He therefore used his mobile phone to ring when they were already well on their way. With the lights flashing and the siren blaring Peiperová was experiencing the exhilaration of driving at around 140 km per hour while Slonský attempted to remain calm in the passenger seat.

He explained to Rajka that they were on their way to Holice to question Captain Forman about his knowledge of the explosion and recapitulated the discussion he had shared with Peiperová in his office.

'Do you think Forman is psychic?' asked Rajka.

'I don't think anyone is psychic,' said Slonský. 'Some people are just good guessers, I suppose.'

'I doubt that Forman was able to guess that there might be an explosion.'

'No,' agreed Slonský. 'I have an idea about that but I mustn't prejudge the interrogation. Captain Forman and I will have a nice little chat about it.'

'Good. Then you'll arrest him for being some kind of accessory to murder and bring him back to Prague?'

'That's the plan.'

'Excellent. Then I needn't traipse over there to kick his arse when I can stay here in the comfort of my own office and have his arse delivered to me.'

'Do you want it still attached?'

'Probably best if it is. There are standards, Slonský.'


'Sirens off now, lass. I don't want them to know what's about to hit them,' Slonský told Peiperová as they got closer.

'What are we going to do, sir?'

'We don't know how many officers are involved in this, so it's just possible we might be outnumbered, but with surprise on our side perhaps we can have Forman in cuffs and out of there before others notice. The whole thing is going to require delicate handling. You'd better let me take the lead.'

Slonský's approach suggested to Peiperová that whichever dictionary he used at school it had a different definition of "delicate" to hers. Pushing open the station door he waved his ID at the sergeant on the desk and kept walking.

'We know our way, thank you.'

Holice was not a big station. In fact, it looked rather like a large house if you disregarded the absence of ground floor windows. Slonský led the way to Forman's office. The door was already open so when Forman glanced up he knew what was coming.

'No coffee for us, thank you,' Slonský announced to Forman's secretary, before marching into the office and kicking the door shut behind him.

'What is the mean—?' began Forman.

'Shut up,' barked Slonský. 'I need to do the formal bit first. You are being interviewed under caution. You are not obliged to say anything but anything you do say may be taken down and given in evidence. Co-operation with our enquiries may be reflected in the sentence you receive. It will certainly be reflected in the number of teeth you still have when I leave this room.'

Peiperová had spotted Forman's holster hanging on a peg and retrieved it just in case Forman had ideas about shooting his way out.

'I don't know what you're talking about,' Forman muttered unconvincingly, but the pallor of his complexion told a different story.

'Cats in the belfry.'

'What's that supposed to mean?'

'You know what I'm talking about, don't you, Peiperová?'

'Yes, sir,' the young officer agreed, recognising the reference to the story that Lukas had told but having no idea how it applied to what was unfolding before her.

'Get yourself a chair, lass, we're going to be here a little while. Now, maybe you do things differently out here in the sticks, but where I come from we find the best way to run a police interview is for the police to ask the questions while the suspect confines themselves to answering. In full, and damn quick. Clear?'

'I demand to know what this is about!' Forman blustered.

'Very fair question,' Slonský agreed. 'This is about seven to fourteen years behind bars, give or take. That's the going rate for accessory to murder, I think. Maybe a bit extra for malfeasance in a public office or whatever the prosecutors are calling it these days. Being naughty in a uniform, that kind of thing. Though I imagine in a small town like this the public disgrace of being marched out to the car in handcuffs and driven slowly around with the sirens going full blast will be the worst bit. Not for your family, of course. They'll probably have to move when all the right-thinking citizens give them the cold shoulder. Perhaps if you're lucky they'll let you know where they've moved to, but I wouldn't count on it. We both know what happens when wives face a decade or more on their own, don't we?'

Forman was shocked that it had come to this. His hands were trembling, causing him to drop them below the desk in a belated attempt to avoid Slonský's seeing them.

'I'm not going to question you in full here. We're going to be rounding up a few people and I hate repeating myself, so let's just talk about your experience of traffic control.'

Forman was a stout man. Although part of that was middle-aged spread, he had always been square in shape, but now he seemed to crumple inwards as if Slonský's old grandmother had been on to something when she told him that if you unknotted your navel all the air would escape.

'That's what this is about, isn't it?' Slonský continued. 'You knew that gun was going to be moved at six o'clock so you went up there to divert any traffic and see them out to the main road.'

Forman began to cry quietly. Slonský could see that his resistance was about to break and allowed the silence to oppress him. 'It wasn't meant to be like this. It's all that damn fool Veselý's fault.'

'There's no law against being stupid, thank God, or our jails would be crammed and Parliament would be empty,' Slonský opined.

'Nearly forty years that blasted gun has been hidden here and he had to flush it out.'

'Tell me how you knew about it.'

Forman blew his nose. He was telling his story to his desk top, unwilling to look into Slonský's accusing eyes. 'My wife's father was one of the men who were detached to hide the gun in 1968. He would never speak about what happened then, but when he was dying a couple of years ago he told his sons and one of them told her. And my wife believes there should be no secrets between a man and his wife, so she told me.'

'And who are those sons?'

'My wife is the youngest one in the family. Her middle brother is the mayor.'

'It sounds as if her brother is good at keeping secrets, then, because I assume he didn't tell his own deputy.'

'No, he didn't trust Veselý to keep it quiet. Veselý chatters like a parrot. You can't tell him anything confidential.'

'So when Veselý began to clear the site for his dream development, there was a risk he would stumble across the gun?' Slonský asked.

'It was in a large barn not far from the cottages. We had no idea that he was planning to start building already. He hadn't even got all the money together, but one day he just sent in the bulldozers. We only had a couple of hours to find somewhere for it.'

'So you moved it in broad daylight?'

Forman shook his head. 'We arranged for someone from the council to stop the bulldozers over a procedural technicality. We knew they had the right papers and that Veselý would soon get them going again, but he was out of town for the day, so it gave us that night to move the gun. We couldn't think where to put it until someone mentioned that Miss Valachová's field was empty. We went by a roundabout route and concealed it as best we could with canvas and camouflage netting. But it couldn't stay there. We had to find another place for it. It took us a while but the mayor's brother owned a disused coal yard. We thought if we could get it there we could build a shelter for it.'

'We've checked the coal yard. There's no gun there,' Slonský insisted.

Forman sighed. 'No, the idiot who was driving it couldn't find anywhere out of sight. There was too much debris lying around, so he turned round and came back out again. He eventually found somewhere to put it, but I don't know where.'

'There's an artillery piece in private hands and you're not curious about where it is?'

'I just wanted it gone, Captain. It was a daft idea to hide it in 1968 and it hasn't got any better since.'

'Why wasn't it handed to the Czech Army after the Wall came down?'

'I asked that very question. Old Nerad said that he couldn't make that decision alone. He wanted to get the men together again so they could discuss it. But he could never find them all. I suspect he was probably the last of them, but until he could prove that, he went on fantasising about a reunion.'

'Whereas if he'd asked you, you'd have been able to track them down using — or misusing — State resources.'

'Yes.'

Forman forced a grim smile. 'I don't think you'd have criticised me for doing that, would you, in the circumstances?'

'No, I don't think I would. But obstructing a murder enquiry is a very different thing. So, you've agreed to help them move the gun. And you're going to move it on Liberation Day because then you can risk moving it in daylight.'

'It's really difficult to drive it at night. The driver's visibility isn't good.'

'Hence why he flattened a tree on the way.'

Forman smoothed his brow with his hand. He clearly had not heard about that.

'You see,' Slonský continued. 'Peiperová here questioned the old man who lives in the cottage down the road — what's his name?'

'Jiří Jeníček, sir.'

'That's the man. He told us your car was parked in the middle of the road a couple of hundred metres from the field. If you'd been investigating an explosion why wouldn't you drive right up to the field? And why not park it neatly by the side? The obvious answer was that you were deliberately blocking the road.'

Forman nodded. 'I was going to walk past to the top of the road and stop the traffic there too. But while I was explaining that to my nephew and his cronies Lieutenant Sedlák turned up.'

'And Sedlák wanted to know why you, a police officer, were helping a bunch of private individuals move a piece of artillery.'

'He was going to report it at once. I argued that the game was up and they should just hand it over, but my nephew waved the gun out and it set off on its route. That left me and

Sedlák's party arguing in the road. My nephew suggested we go into the field to continue the discussion away from the attention of anyone who might pass by. When we were all in the field he snatched my gun and told them to sit down. One of his colleagues had some cable ties in his tool kit, so they were tied up. I asked what they were going to do with them, but my nephew just smiled and said that there was only one answer. He told me to make myself scarce and he'd return my gun later. I protested that I didn't want my gun used to kill people. He took the bullets out and handed it back. I'd only got about halfway to the car when I heard the explosion. As God is my witness, I didn't know they had grenades. I thought when I got my gun back I'd saved their lives.' He covered his face and sobbed.

'Now,' Slonský continued, 'tell us about the cover-up. You made no effort to help us investigate the murder because you already knew who'd done it. According to our pathologist one of the murderers may have been injured in the blast.'

Forman nodded. 'The mechanic. He was slow leaving the field with the weight of his tool kit and took some shrapnel in his back.'

'Did he get medical help?'

'I got a local nurse to look at him. We told her the mechanic had been passing by the field when the explosion happened. It was a bit messy, but no real harm done.'

'What happened in the field was more than "a bit messy" though, wasn't it? It was carnage. And you knew who did it.'

Peiperová was tentatively raising and lowering her hand to attract his attention.

'Do you need a pee, girl?' Slonský snapped.

'No, sir, it's just — Officer Navrátil mentioned someone called Nerad in his report the other day.'

'Not to me, he didn't. Have you been getting reports of your own?'

'No, sir, not really. He made some notes before Captain Lukas' retirement and I said I'd type them up for him.'

'This would be young Nerad, I suppose?'

'Yes, sir. He runs a group called Our Home.'

'That's my nephew,' Forman interrupted.

'So in addition to murdering a police officer and three others your nephew is hatching some plot against the security of the state.'

'No! Never! David is a patriot,' Forman insisted.

Slonský stood up and leaned over the desk so that his face was only centimetres from Forman's. 'One of my best men has been working undercover infiltrating that group. If he comes to harm I will personally dangle your balls over a beehive and give it a good kick to stir up the inhabitants. Now, we'd better go and arrest your nephew, hadn't we?'

Forman stood up and donned his jacket.

'You're under arrest for obstructing the police in the conduct of an enquiry. Do you understand?' Slonský asked.

Forman nodded again.

'I need you to say yes.'

'Yes,' croaked Forman.

'Good. Let's not make a drama out of this. If you promise not to try to escape I won't put the cuffs on till we're in the car.'

'Thank you,' Forman whispered. 'I appreciate your consideration.'

They left the office together, Peiperová bringing up the rear.

'I'm just going out,' Forman told his secretary. 'Please cancel my appointments.'

'Until when?' she asked.

'About 2025,' Slonský replied.

They settled into the car, Peiperová driving while Slonský and Forman sat in the back.

'Where to, sir?'

'Tricky. We need Captain Forman to identify his nephew. Let's swing through town on the way to Pardubice to see if we can spot Nerad. Then we'll collect Doležal and he can look after one of the suspects while I manage the other. I don't trust the other police in Pardubice.'

'I'll try the railway station first, sir. If someone at Pardubice revealed Navrátil's identity to Nerad they'd probably want to stop him leaving town.'

'Good idea.'

The train station was only two blocks away so Peiperová did not need directions. As they turned off the main road a young man who was talking urgently to another suddenly broke off upon seeing the police car and ran into the station.

'That's David,' said Forman, rather unnecessarily.

Slonský realised his dilemma. Chasing a suspect is much more difficult when you're handcuffed to another one.

'You follow, Peiperová! Forman, out!'

Within a few moments Slonský had released himself from the handcuffs and attached Forman to the steel frame of a fence instead.

'Stay here!' he told him, even more unnecessarily.

Peiperová was tall, fit and fast. The man to whom Nerad had been speaking moved as if to impede her path but she swatted him aside by driving her shoulder into his side and kept running. The man stumbled but had just regained his balance when Slonský caught up and hooked his ankle with his leg. When he sprawled on the ground Slonský stamped on his knee.

'That's so I'll be able to identify you when we come back,' he explained.

Slonský had reached the platform just in time to see Peiperová on the far side of the tracks running away from him. The station was just a couple of tracks and a platform with no fencing or barriers, so Nerad had been able to run across the track and disappear into the streets opposite. Slonský could only hope that Peiperová had remembered that Nerad could be dangerous.

He turned back and headed for the car. The young man was sitting on the kerb rubbing his sore knee when Slonský hoisted him by the collar of his jacket.

'Come along, sunshine,' he said. 'You'll be company for Captain Forman.'

Unfortunately Slonský only had one pair of handcuffs so he began by cuffing both their right arms. That would make it harder for them to run away, especially since the cable was still wrapped around the railing.

In her haste to chase after Nerad, Peiperová had left the car keys in the ignition.

'Fortunately even in Holice nobody dares to steal a police car,' Slonský mused as he climbed inside and parked himself in the driver's seat. He turned the car round and wound down the window. 'You two are going to have to amuse yourselves while I find Peiperová. Try to play nicely together.' And then he was gone.

Doležal ran into the café and looked about him. He understood why Navrátil had not shared useful information like the place where he was living, but it made it hard to rescue him if you did not know where to look. He asked the woman behind the counter whether the student had been in. She said he had not, though given that she knew Doležal to be a policeman, she would have told him that even if it had not been true.

Doležal thanked her and turned to leave, only to see the door open and Klaberský standing there. He had a gun.

'I think we need to have a little chat,' he said. 'Just you, me and Captain Vondra.'

Navrátil's plan was simple. He would make himself as inconspicuous as possible, then he would find a place of safety, and finally he would ring Poznar to get himself collected. Although he did not know it, Poznar had already decided that things were not going well. Since Navrátil was plainly taking the instruction to contact him only in extreme circumstances very literally, Poznar rang him instead.

'Where are you?' Poznar asked.

'There's a farm we searched to the north of town. We were taken in by helicopter so I'm having trouble getting my bearings on the ground, but that's where I'm heading.'

'I'll call a map up,' Poznar said. 'Anything else you can recall about it?'

'We were there because the gun had flattened a tree. It couldn't get across a small bridge so it turned in a coal yard.'

'Okay, got it. At least, I can see the bridge and the yard. Tell me where you are.'

Navrátil described his route from the church.

'Can you see a gate?' asked Poznar.

'There's one across the road,' Navrátil replied, 'about fifty metres in front of me.'

'First turning to the right once you're passed it, then left at the top and you should see the road you want to your right again. I'm coming to get you so stay out of sight until we arrive. I'll park at the coal yard and walk back down the road.'

As she ran Peiperová glanced about her in the hope of seeing Navrátil. She had to trust that when he saw her running in uniform he would have the wit to come to her because her main focus had to be on finding Nerad.

Nerad was looking out for Navrátil himself. He had given the police the slip and paused to gather his breath in an alleyway before resuming his search. He could hear running and flattened himself against the wall in the hope of escaping notice. A blue flash ran past the end of the alley, then, after a couple of seconds, Peiperová returned.

'You're under arrest,' she called.

Nerad grabbed her arm as she attempted to draw her gun, wrenched it out of her hand and kicked it away along the alley. She managed to break free and they stood opposite each other a couple of metres apart.

'What are you going to do now, little girl?' he grinned.

Peiperová relaxed. She left her aggressive crouching posture and stood upright. Fixing Nerad with her cool blue eyes her gaze roamed over his face. 'You've got nice skin,' she said. 'Do you moisturize?'

Nerad took in those eyes, the soft voice, its admiring tone, and was still processing them as her foot thudded into his scrotum and his world seemed to end in a great explosion.

Slonský looked at the three men chained to the fence.

'Ordinarily I'd call the police,' he said, 'but I can't trust the police here. Where the hell is Doležal when you want him? He's not answering his phone.'

'I'll run back to the station and get someone to take the two young men to the cells,' Peiperová volunteered.

'No, we can't leave Nerad here in Holice. They can take Hopalong, though, and they can bring another car and a couple of beefy lads to give us a hand.'

Peiperová ran off, leaving Slonský standing over the three men as a crowd gathered.

A middle-aged man with a little moustache addressed him. 'You there! Are you in charge?'

'That's why I've got the gun.'

'I hope you're someone official. That's a police officer you're pointing that at, you know.'

'I guessed that. The uniform is a bit of a giveaway. I'm one too, so I've seen it before.' He flipped his wallet open to show his badge.

There was a gasp from the bystanders at the realisation that their police chief was attached to a fence in his own town.

'Is this a training exercise?' the officious man continued, 'because I don't think you should be running around a public area with firearms.'

'I'll ask the criminals I meet to bear that in mind, sir,' Slonský replied. 'I doubt they'll play ball, but it's worth a try. Suggestions from the public are always welcome.'

Slonský's phone rang, so he took it out to see who was calling. Seeing the name Rajka on the screen, he took the call.

'How's it going, Slonský?'

'Very well. I've got Captain Forman with me now. We're getting on famously.'

'Good. I assume there's no chance that you'll be bringing him back in the next hour or two?'

'Unfortunately I think we have some further business to attend to at this end.'

'Police business?'

'Involving the police, yes,' Slonský said cautiously.

There was a pause. 'And there are just the two of you?'

'That's right.'

'And you're planning to arrest and hold four police officers? Just the two of you?'

'We've got two others in custody but Peiperová has gone for some help at the local station.'

Rajka sighed. 'And those officers can be trusted?'

'We'll soon know. But I wasn't planning to give their old boss to them to look after because you want to see him in Prague.'

'I'll tell you what,' said Rajka. 'Why don't I get in the car and come to you?'

'That would be appreciated,' Slonský said. 'And could you bring a good supply of handcuffs?'


Doležal's back slammed into the wall of the workshop.

'So what was your little snitch friend doing here?' Klaberský demanded, not for the first time.

'I've told you, I don't know.'

'Our informant says you met up in a café in Holice soon after he arrived.'

'That was just coincidence. We happened to be in the same place.'

'Just like you both happened to go to the same retirement?'

'Captain Lukas was in command of both of us. But I don't work with Navrátil. He works for Slonský.'

Klaberský might have overlooked this piece of intelligence but Vondra tugged at his sleeve and pulled him to one side for an urgent discussion. It was clear that Vondra had no wish to antagonise Slonský unnecessarily, whereas Klaberský saw this as an opportunity to wreak some kind of revenge.

Klaberský shrugged Vondra off and addressed himself to Doležal once again.

'I warned you to keep your nose out of things, but it seems you're not much of a listener.'

He swung a length of wood which cracked across Doležal's kneecap. Doležal's leg collapsed beneath him and he dropped to one knee. The plank circled again and smacked into his ribs, causing him to curl up in pain, but this did not stop the beating. Again and again Klaberský sent the wood driving into Doležal's body until the screaming stopped and there was no more fun to be had.


The young officer approached Peiperová as she was speaking to the sergeant to get the men Slonský wanted.

'May I have a word?' he said.

'Can it wait?'

'I don't think so. It's about a car. It's illegally parked.'

'That's not a Crime matter,' Peiperová replied.

'No, but it's registered to the police in Prague.'

Peiperová could not think whose it could be. The officer produced a digital camera and found the image.

'It's been there over three hours with no sign of the officer.'

The unmarked police cars did not differ much from each other, so Peiperová was no wiser until an idea came to her.

'Lieutenant Doležal!'

'Sorry?'

'He drives a car like that. He's on secondment to Pardubice, but he isn't picking up his phone. I wonder if something has happened to him?'

'No accident has been reported.'

'You don't know Doležal like I do. He wouldn't park illegally by choice. He follows the rules meticulously. Where is this?'

'Near the café.'

It all fell into place. Doležal had discovered that someone in the police knew Navrátil's identity. He had rung Slonský to warn him to get Navrátil out, then he must have driven over to Holice to see if he could find Navrátil himself. But if something had happened to Doležal perhaps it had happened to Navrátil too?

Peiperová wanted to vomit. She loved her work and she had braved some tough times since coming to Prague but right at that moment she wanted to drop to the floor and empty her guts. This was too much to cope with.

The young officer put his arm around her shoulders. 'Are you okay?' he asked.

Peiperová nodded, gritted her teeth and fanned her face to compose herself. 'Please come with me. I need you to repeat this to Captain Slonský.'

Slonský listened intently. 'So you think Doležal may be with Navrátil?'

'I think Lieutenant Doležal may be in trouble, wherever he is, sir,' Peiperová answered, though she could not disguise her concern about her fiancé's welfare.

Slonský handed his phone to Peiperová. 'I can't work that thing. Find me Poznar's number and dial it for me.'

Peiperová did as she was bidden and handed the phone back.

'Poznar, have you heard anything about Navrátil yet?'

'Yes, he's in a place of safety. I won't tell you where it is in case anyone is listening in, but I'm on my way now to collect him.'

'Good. He didn't mention Lieutenant Doležal being with him?'

'Doležal? No, not a word. Should he be?'

'Nobody has seen him since he rang this morning to say Navrátil's cover was blown. And his empty car has been found. I'm concerned.'

'I would be too. When I've collected Navrátil shall I come and find you?'

'Only if it's safe for him, otherwise get him out of here. We'll manage — but thanks for the offer.'


Slonský had divided the party between the two cars. Forman was in his car, whilst Nerad and the hobbling man were placed in the other to be taken to the cells in Pardubice where the Holice police would guard them until Slonský had them replaced.

'I hate not knowing who can be trusted,' Slonský muttered. His phone rang again. 'Not now, Mucha!' he snapped.

'Yes, now! I've got a phone number for you to ring, and you will ring it as soon as I put the phone down. Have you got a pen?'

'Yes, but no paper.'

Forman helpfully handed him his notebook.

'Fire away.' Slonský copied down the number. 'Who is it and why am I ringing them?'

'It's some guy called Staněk and he says he knows where Doležal is, but he won't tell anyone but you.'

'Right. Get off the line, Mucha, this is important.' Slonský dialled the number as instructed.

'Staněk.'

'Lieutenant, this is Slonský speaking.'

'I'm glad you've called. I've got your man to the hospital in Pardubice but there's only me here and I daren't leave him unguarded. Can you get me some help?'

'How is he?'

'Not good. It's touch and go. They gave him a terrific beating.'

'You've done well, Staněk. I won't forget this. We'll get there as fast as we can.'

Slonský rang off, instructed Peiperová to head for the hospital in Pardubice, and then asked her for simple instructions to find Poznar in his contacts list. He dialled and explained what had happened.

'Leave it with me,' said Poznar. 'Help within the hour.'

Slonský rang off. 'At last. A policeman I can trust.'

Peiperová shot him a look. 'A policeperson, I mean. And present company … never mind.'


Slonský knew he and Staněk were going to get along. For a start, Staněk said very little. When Slonský, Forman and Peiperová found the ward they saw Staněk standing guard outside the room. He did not greet them with any more than a cursory nod.

'Doc's in there now. There's some internal bleeding they've had to deal with but they think it's stopped,' he said.

'Is he going to be all right?'

'They won't predict anything.'

Slonský slapped the wall in annoyance. Keen as he was to get rid of Doležal he did not want it to happen this way. 'How did you find him?'

'Got the technical department to trace his phone.'

'Good to about a fifty metre circle. And then?'

'Klaberský has a workshop where he works on his motor bikes. It seemed a good place to start.'

'And no doubt you saw something that justified you breaking in?'

'It wasn't locked.'

'Really? That'll make life easier when we take them to court. When you say "not locked" do you mean unlocked, or not effectively locked?'

'The front door was locked. I entered through the side door.'

'Which they must have overlooked when locking up.'

Staněk did not intend to lie so he just said nothing.

'Tell me about Vondra and Klaberský,' Slonský continued.

'How do you mean?'

'What are they like?'

Staněk shrugged. 'Vondra's a dinosaur. Klaberský's a raptor.'

'Have they ever shown extreme political tendencies before?'

'Vondra harks back to the old days. He's not political. He just doesn't want 1968 to happen again. Klaberský's only cause is Klaberský.'

'But they've frustrated the murder inquiry into what happened to your colleague Sedlák.'

Staněk stood detached, eyes fixed in front, like a sentry. 'That's why I'm here now.'

'If you know anything about the circumstances of Sedlák's death, this is the time to share it.'

'I don't. Except that the two of them were with me.'

'At six o'clock on Liberation Day?'

'I can't swear to the hour. But too late to have made it to Holice anyway. Vondra likes us to put on a bit of a show on Liberation Day. Full uniform. Make the police visible to the public. So we were in Pernštýnské Square that afternoon, all of us.'

'But not Sedlák?'

'Sedlák asked whether we were on duty, because if we were, he'd expect to be paid. Vondra said we weren't, so Sedlák said he was entitled to take the holiday. After all, he didn't live in Pardubice like the rest of us.'

'But you look after the east of the region?'

'I come from Litomysl, about fifty kilometres to the south east, but I got fed up with driving back and forth to hand in reports. Besides, the area idea is just a basic way of dividing work. There's less crime in my patch so I was spending most of my time here anyway.'

The doors opened and Poznar entered, followed by a little priest. It was doubtful whether Slonský would have recognised him if a nearby policewoman had not run to embrace him. He kissed her in a way that is not normally associated with priests, causing Staněk's mouth to drop open.

'It's a Prague thing,' Slonský explained, clapping him on the shoulder, before striding forward to speak to Poznar. 'Where's the help?' he asked.

Poznar looked sheepish. 'The duty squadron is on an exercise. I've called out the standby but they'll probably be another half hour or so.'

'Can they land away from the hospital? I've got an idea.'

'You don't have to have ideas now. You've already been promoted,' Poznar pointed out.

'We need to flush Vondra and Klaberský out so we know where they are. But they won't come into the trap if they know the commandos are around.'

Poznar sucked his teeth. 'Is this a hare-brained idea you're having, or a completely mad one?'

'Does it matter?'

'It'll matter at my court martial.'

'It's only slightly loopy.' Slonský beckoned Staněk to join them. 'Staněk, I want you to call Vondra. Tell him you were called by someone reporting an assault. You discovered it was Doležal so you brought him here. Fortunately, Doležal is recovering well and you expect it'll be possible to question him soon.'

Poznar understood now. 'So they'll come running to try to ensure that Doležal doesn't talk.'

'I hope so. And I hope they're not too far away so they won't have time to think before they get here.'

Staněk nodded and went to make his call somewhere quieter.

'Is Navrátil all right?' Slonský enquired.

'Bit shaken,' Poznar replied, 'but he'll do. He's a resourceful lad. He's a bit worried about having to explain what he was doing to the priest whose spare outfit he stole, but otherwise he's okay. And he's given me some useful information about Our Home.'

Slonský beckoned Officer Peiperová to him, which meant that Captain Forman had to come too, since they were handcuffed together now.

'I think they'll smell a rat if they see Captain Forman handcuffed to you. You can't sit in the car in case they see you, but find somewhere in the hospital to keep out of sight. I'll call you when the coast is clear.'

Poznar was making his call to ask the helicopter to land as inconspicuously as possible. There was a small airport at Pardubice where a helicopter landing would not be unusual, so that was nominated. Since it was around five kilometres away, they were told to commandeer taxis. Poznar was concerned with one aspect of the plan. 'They're police officers, Slonský. They'll be armed.'

'I know. So we have to take them by surprise and disarm them. Have you got a weapon?'

'Of course. Have you?'

'Yes. I just haven't got it with me.'

'What?'

'I put it in the glove compartment of the car in case Forman tried to snatch it. His is there too.'

Poznar pointed at the only available person. 'He'll get it for you.'

'Navrátil? There's one small problem. Peiperová has the car keys, and we don't know where she is.'

Further debate was stifled as the doors swung open and Klaberský marched in, Vondra following behind at something of a trot. Klaberský looked through the observation window in the door as if checking that it really was Doležal in there.

'I'm glad you got him here,' Klaberský said to Staněk. The sheer effrontery of it made Slonský's blood pressure rise. 'How about if Captain Vondra relieves you and then I can take the next shift?'

'I don't think so,' said Slonský. 'We don't normally let police officers guard victims they've attempted to kill.'

'What rubbish is this?'

'We don't actually need Doležal's evidence so bumping him off wouldn't help you.'

Poznar had drawn his gun, but Klaberský grabbed a nurse and held her in front of him as a shield as he retreated towards the doors.

'Don't be a fool!' Vondra called. 'It's over.'

'I'm not going to jail,' Klaberský yelled. 'Not now, not ever.' He backed through the door taking a quick glance to check that the path was clear. Slonský restrained Poznar from chasing after him. There was no need. Lurking behind the doors

Slonský could see a little priest wielding a heavy fire extinguisher.

Navrátil swung it smoothly. It cracked into Klaberský's head and he slumped to the ground. Unfortunately Navrátil had somehow pulled the pin out and foam was filling the corridor, so that the nurse had to drop to her knees and lift Klaberský's head free of it. Poznar raced forward to grab Klaberský's gun while Slonský did the same to Vondra.

It was at this moment that Major Rajka turned the corner. He took in the nurse cradling a police officer's head, the priest still holding the assault weapon and the corridor full of foam.

'Well, everything seems to be in order here,' he said.

# Chapter 16

'This is extremely embarrassing,' said Slonský.

'Yes, sir. Sorry, sir,' Peiperová said again.

'What were you thinking of?'

'He said he needed the toilet, sir. I obviously couldn't go in there with him, so I had to take the cuffs off. And there wasn't a male officer free to go instead or to check for escape routes.'

The hospital maintenance crew had dismantled as much of the window as they could but they still could not free Forman, who had attempted to squeeze through and was now wedged by his belly with his head dangling downwards.

'How did he think he was going to get down two storeys?' Peiperová asked.

'I don't think he gave it an awful lot of thought, Peiperová. Maybe he was so desperate to avoid your company that diving head first onto concrete seemed a good option.'

The firefighters had managed to raise their ladder until one of them could take the weight of Forman's shoulders. Slowly they eased him back inside, centimetre by centimetre, until he was able to get his shoulders and arms back through the window. As soon as he did so, Peiperová reapplied the handcuffs.

Forman was returned to earth, allowing the blood to leave his face, which was not an attractive colour. He adjusted his disordered uniform and had the grace to look apologetic. 'I'm sorry,' he said. 'I didn't mean to cause any trouble.'

Slonský sighed. 'I know. But it's a bit hard to give you credit for co-operation when you try to do a runner. Especially with an OII officer in the building at the time.'

They returned to the corridor where Rajka was waiting for them.

'Jesus Maria, that was funny!' he said. 'I've got several photos on my phone. Of course, they'll have to make my word for it that it's Forman's backside wedged in the window. Still, it made the trip to Pardubice worthwhile.'

'How is Klaberský?' asked Slonský.

'Awake but sore. Where do priests learn to thump people like that?'

'He's not a real priest,' Slonský explained. 'He's planning to marry Officer Peiperová here and the church has rules about that.'

'I can see that celibacy might be a challenge,' Rajka agreed, causing Peiperová to blush.

'And he's broken one of the other commandments too. He stole the priest rig.'

'I imagine the church takes a dim view of that too. Of course, OII has rules about police officers stealing stuff,' Rajka said, 'but I don't think we need to know about this.'

Peiperová relaxed.

'Unless the priest makes a formal complaint,' Rajka continued.

'Navrátil is on his way to return the stolen goods right now,' Slonský confirmed. 'He's not looking forward to it. We can only send him to jail for a while but it seems that priests can sentence you to an eternity of little devils tickling the soles of your feet with goose feathers.'

Rajka put a brotherly arm round Slonský's shoulders. 'It's been a grand day out, but how about we all get back to Prague and reconvene in the morning to compare notes?'

'I was just thinking the same thing,' said Slonský. 'I'm missing civilisation already.'

One of the advantages of losing Peiperová to the Director of Criminal Police was that she was able to persuade him to let Slonský have the use of the conference room for the morning, so Slonský, Peiperová, Navrátil, Klinger, Rajka and Poznar were sitting around a highly polished table drinking coffee.

'I didn't know we had cups with the police logo on them,' said Navrátil.

'It's probably to stop anyone stealing them,' Slonský answered. 'It might be an idea if the Catholic church did that with its cassocks.'

Navrátil coloured. 'The priest was actually very nice about it.'

'I'm pleased to hear that,' Slonský replied. 'The people of the Pardubice Region must be getting a bit fed up with seeing police officers in handcuffs.'

'They won't see them for a while,' Rajka interrupted. 'They haven't got many more to arrest.'

'I've had a word with the Director of Criminal Police before the meeting. They're going to offer Doležal Vondra's job. It'll mean a promotion to captaincy. Of course, we don't know whether he'll take it, but I think he might.'

'But he's not going to be back at work for a while, is he, sir?' Peiperová enquired.

'The doctors say he's responding well to treatment now. The pressure in his brain has returned to normal and they're hopeful he'll make a good recovery. Of course you can't take a beating like he took and not expect consequences, but let's hope they're minimal. In the meantime Staněk will be acting captain. We'll have to give them some extra help until they recruit to replace Klaberský and Sedlák, but I'm sending Rada there on a permanent posting. It's not what I'd planned, but he probably didn't want to work for the Border Police anyway. And if Doležal isn't fit for active duty, Captain Lukas suggested

I might find him a role with the Police Academy as an instructor. The police look after their own.'

'That's why we got into this mess,' Rajka suggested.

'There's a right way and a wrong way to do it,' agreed Slonský. 'My way is better than theirs.'

'So,' said Poznar, 'are you going to explain what has been going here?'

Slonský opened the folder in front of him and read from the top sheet. 'It says here "Conspiracy. Noun. An agreement between two or more people to commit an act prohibited by law or to commit a lawful act by means prohibited by law." The trouble here is that we have overlapping conspiracies. And I have to thank Captain Lukas for reminding me about the cats in the belfry, because frankly until I heard that I didn't have a clue what was going on.' He extracted a gruesome photograph from the folder. 'This is where it all started. Four men killed in an explosion. They were killed because they stumbled across the gun being moved. Captain Forman was, of course, implicated in that. It suited him to concoct a story about accidental detonation of a shell by people with metal detectors, and that's what he reported to Pardubice. That case would have been closed if it had not been for Dr Novák's discovery that the forensics were not consistent with that story. Forman was unco-operative because he had wanted no questions asked about the gun. How is the search for the gun going, by the way?'

'Nerad is being unhelpful,' said Poznar, 'but the chap with the sore knee gave us the name of the driver of the gun on its last journey. If he had given it a bit quicker he wouldn't now have two sore knees. And the driver was quick to come up with an address once he realised we were serious about wanting it. As I pointed out to him, we don't go round kicking people's front doors in at one in the morning unless we're really keen to hear what they have to say.'

'So where is it now?'

'The army have taken possession of it. I spoke to the officer who led the retrieval team. He says it has been well maintained but they'll give it a good home.'

'So that explains the deaths. Forman will testify that Nerad either threw the grenade or knows who did, because there were only two possible perpetrators in the field when it happened. That brings us to David Nerad.'

Poznar had been interrogating him, so picked up the thread. 'Nerad's plan was detailed in a draft speech we found notes for. He was going to take the gun to Prague and lob a few shells into the city while the American President was being formally greeted. It didn't matter what the shells hit so long as they hit something. Nerad would then argue that the current crop of politicians had failed in their duty to keep the Czech people safe and that a "more patriotic" government was needed. He had identified twelve to fifteen candidates to stand at the next election. He was one, of course, and you'll be pleased to hear you were on it too, Navrátil. Or, more accurately, Michal Ondráček was. With a block of ten or so deputies he could influence the next government, in which, of course, he would play a major role as Our Home's leader.'

Slonský was concerned. 'Sounds like he could plead insanity and get off with it.'

'Not with the detailed planning he had done,' Poznar countered.

'So the plan to use the gun was his decision and none of the others knew?' Slonský asked.

'At present, we have no indication that anyone else knew who was connected with the original diversion. Some members of Our Home knew what was going to happen but probably only in general terms. The driver, for example, says he only knew he was going to take it for a drive on 4th June, but not where they would be going,' Poznar replied.

'You see, this is where the cats in the belfry came in,' Slonský continued. 'If the target was the American President's visit, I couldn't see why they would take it out of hiding so early. What possible trigger could have led to that? But then it occurred to me, having heard Captain Lukas, that the trigger may not have been the one that they had planned for. And when Klinger returned from interviewing Veselý with the news that he had suddenly and spontaneously started clearing the site to persuade his new Russian pals to get their hands in their pockets, the idea began to form that cats had just kicked the bell.'

Klinger took up the story. 'Veselý's plan is now dead. The Russian investors were indeed planning to launder their criminal profits by investing in the mall. They would cash out the leisure complex quite soon, then begin to demand repayments of the remainder. If it profited, Veselý would be glad to buy them out. If not, he stood the loss. Either way, they'd have money in their hands with a clean provenance.'

'You see,' Slonský explained, 'Veselý had no interest in changing the government. Nerad had no plans to invest in a mall. So you can't really call it a conspiracy.'

'But what about Klaberský and Vondra, sir?' asked Peiperová. 'Where do they come in?'

'After the explosion, Forman told Vondra what had really happened in order to get his help in covering it up. Vondra told Klaberský. That's why they were so hostile to Doležal; they thought he had been sent to reopen the enquiry. They saw to it that any information Doležal shared with them was discredited or destroyed. That's why he didn't tell them what he had heard about the cottages. He was beginning to suspect that they were being obstructive. But whereas Vondra just wanted to please the local bigwigs and have a quiet life, Klaberský saw a great opportunity. Major Rajka and I visited his house on the way back to Prague last night and helped ourselves to a number of documents there.'

Rajka rubbed his hands together with relish before taking up the story. 'Klaberský knew there was a big gun around. He knew that David Nerad was somehow implicated, though probably not that he had actually thrown the grenade. He reasoned that Nerad wouldn't play second fiddle to anyone and therefore was likely to be the ringleader of whatever plot was in contemplation. He also guessed one or two of the young men around Holice known to the police who might become involved in Nerad's plan, our friend with the sore knees being one of them. Klaberský twisted their arms to keep him informed and to agitate for ever more daring plans. At the same time they were feeding Klaberský bits of evidence. His plan was to appear to be supportive but at the last moment he would turn hero and foil the plot. It wouldn't matter that they had never intended to harm the American President, because Klaberský could make a good case that they must have done. As a national hero, "the man who saved Prague" would be set on a rapid course upwards in the police.'

'But why hurt Doležal?' asked Navrátil.

Slonský answered. 'Because once they discovered that we had you infiltrating the group, and Doležal was able to warn you that your cover was blown, Klaberský's little plot, in which he had invested a lot of time and quite a bit of money, was likely to unravel. If you and Doležal stepped in and arrested Nerad, Klaberský had lost his chance. Not only that, but if his sources talked, his position might be really tricky. Pure, naked fear, lad. If he could stop Doležal reporting what he knew, the arrest might still be his.'

'Did it matter so much to him that he would try to kill a fellow policeman to get the collar, sir?' Navrátil exclaimed in astonishment.

'Yes, lad, it did. You see, you and Peiperová are doing well. You'll be lieutenants in a year or two and captains not long after, I reckon. But Klaberský had twenty years of lack of achievement under his belt. And he probably looked at Vondra and thought that was what he was destined to turn into. Not an enticing thought.'

'But I thought he'd said he was hoping to get Vondra's job when he retired, sir?' asked Peiperová.

'Hoping, yes; but not certain. And was that enough for him? Head of a team of three operating out of an oversized cupboard in the sticks? We're back to fear. What if he didn't get it? What if they gave it to — say — Sedlák? After all, Sedlák was the oldest and longest-serving lieutenant there. No wonder he wasn't heartbroken when Sedlák was killed.'

'It's still unimaginable, sir,' Navrátil said. 'Not being able to trust other colleagues.'

'Welcome to my world,' said Rajka.

# Chapter 17

The following Sunday, Slonský bought a bunch of flowers for Mrs Lukasová in readiness for their arranged lunch and, in a rare display of romantic feeling, a corsage for Věra which she proudly pinned to her chest. Never mind that it was a lurid violet, a colour she thoroughly detested; it was the thought that counted, she told herself. She gave him a peck on the cheek, then, pausing only to brush his shoulders, straighten his tie and disappear to the kitchen to find a cloth to buff up his toecaps, she led the way out.

They caught the tram like any other middle-aged couple that Sunday in Prague. As it passed one of his favourite bars Slonský looked out fondly, caressing it with his eyes and almost wishing he was there instead; but his duty lay elsewhere.

And he could hardly allow Captain Lukas to be left unsupported with two women and two daughters, could he?

Věra followed his gaze. 'Honestly, Josef, you don't change,' she tutted.

*I'm eight kilos lighter, I'm a captain and I'm going out to lunch with you*, thought Slonský. *That sounds like a hell of a metamorphosis to me.*

# A NOTE TO THE READER

Dear Reader,

Thank you for investing your money and time in my book. For those who worry about this sort of thing, *Lying and Dying* was set in February 2006, *Slaughter and Forgetting* in the following May, and *Death on Duty* in November 2006. This book is set in May 2007.

When I started out I thought Slonský would be a lieutenant until his retirement, but he continues to surprise me even now. I believed that I knew what would happen in books 5 and 6 but now I am not so sure.

The story of the ghost battery is not entirely fiction; that is not to say that it is true, but that rumours about a vanishing big gun had circulated. It is true that the Warsaw Pact satellites varied the composition of their artillery regiments so that it was not impossible that one might have been hidden without the Soviet Union becoming aware of it, but that is a very different thing to saying that anyone ever actually did it.

A second element in the story came to me when I saw an article questioning the provenance of some of the capital for large shopping malls in Central and Eastern Europe. This suggested the idea of a white elephant mall whose major purpose was to launder criminal gains.

If you have enjoyed this novel I'd be really grateful if you would leave a review on **Amazon** and **Goodreads**. I love to hear from readers, so please keep in touch through **Facebook** or **Twitter**, or leave a message on my **website**.

Všechno nejlepší!

Graham Brack

**Sapere Books** is an exciting new publisher of brilliant fiction and popular history.

To find out more about our latest releases and our monthly bargain books visit our website: **saperebooks.com**

Made in the USA
Middletown, DE
23 November 2019

79293890R00149